Edward Hartley Dewart

Songs of Life

A Collection of Poems

Edward Hartley Dewart

Songs of Life
A Collection of Poems

ISBN/EAN: 9783742813978

Manufactured in Europe, USA, Canada, Australia, Japa

Cover: Foto ©Andreas Hilbeck / pixelio.de

Manufactured and distributed by brebook publishing software
(www.brebook.com)

Edward Hartley Dewart

Songs of Life

SONGS OF LIFE:

A Collection of Poems.

BY

EDWARD HARTLEY DEWART.

TORONTO:

DUDLEY & BURNS, PRINTERS.

1869.

PREFACE.

It is natural that an author should have a desire to remove any prejudice, in the minds of his readers, that would prevent him receiving a fair hearing. Yet, the preface of a book is often not read at all—nor the book itself, for that matter. Many are the excuses of authors. Youth, sex, and want of time, are in turn pleaded, in extenuation of imperfections. Frequently the advice of admiring friends is given, as a reason for doing what the author himself deems rather questionable. However much I may need them, I am afraid none of these excuses are available in the present case. Though the kindly judgment of friends has not been without influence, I would be sorry to make them the scape-goat, for any sins of imprudence or presumption, this venture may seem to evince.

It is often said, that of poetry we should read only the best. This may be true; but it is also true, that what may be the best to one, may not be the best for another. Much poetry that is highly lauded by critics, and which unquestionably reveals power and subtlety of thought, can never be appreciated by the great mass of readers; who know no standard of excellence, but the degree in which the sentiments of a writer come home to their hearts, as beautiful or true. Many who have no capacity to enjoy the elaborate and involved sentences, remote and learned allusions, and "deep inwoven harmonies," which delight those who have cultivated their taste, and adjusted their admiration to that standard, may, nevertheless, feel the power of a simple, earnest lyric, which conveys to the heart some truth, never so deeply felt before. Like the planets, that reflect the light of the sun, with a subdued lustre, minor bards may be allowed to stand, as interpreters to the many, of the kingly minds, who dwell in the inaccessible cyries of thought.

These poems make no pretension to elaborate art, inventive genius, or quaint and ingenious word-painting; and may, consequently, be unacceptable to those who deem these essential. But I hope, notwithstanding, that they may not be found devoid of interest to those, who having no theory to maintain, are ready to give a candid and generous reception to any grains of gold, which may be found scattered through them.

The inner spiritual life, which is the theme of several of the pieces in this volume, is a field which contains mines of untold poetic wealth, awaiting the developing hand of genius. A word may be due to those well-meaning, but illiberal persons, who may question the propriety of a minister of religion writing on any, but purely religious subjects. All nature is full of truth and beauty, claiming our regard. Every phase of human life has lessons for thoughtful minds. All who have studied the tendencies and wants of the times, will endorse the sentiment of Dr. ARNOLD, that secular literature, written from a sound Christian stand-point, is needed more, than that which is directly religious.

In submitting these unpretending effusions to Canadian readers, I have only to say, that, should they be received with favor, I hope at some future time, if life and health be spared, to offer them something better worthy of their acceptance.

E. H. D.

INGERSOLL, May 12th, 1869.

CONTENTS.

——⊙——

Songs of the World Without :

Songs of the World Within:

Songs of Home and Heart:

National and Patriotic Pieces :

Miscellaneous Pieces :

ERRATUM.

Page 111, line 9, for "morn" read *moon*.

SONGS OF LIFE.

PROLOGUE.

CHILD of my love, thy sylvan lays contain
 The garner'd thoughts of many a pensive hour;
The gush of gladness and the plaint of pain
 Are vocal here, as they in turn had power
To tone the musings of a pilgrim soul,
While onward journeying to life's common goal.

Here varied flowers are in one wreath united—
 But chiefly natives of the forest wild,
From youth to age, my fancy most delighted;
 Since first I played, a happy, thoughtless child,
Fresh, virgin nature, undefaced by art,
Has whispered rapture thro' my yearning heart.

I weave not Fancy's webs of idle thought,
 Nor twine gay garlands for proud Beauty's brow—
To fashions vain, with deadly poison fraught,
 Should poet-soul with cringing homage bow,
To silver over selfishness and wrong,
With the soft grace and witchery of song?

Why should the Poet's life be vainly given
  'To lullabies, which sing the guilty soul
Asleep, without a living hope of heaven—
  Madly forgetful of life's final goal ?
Or why should he, at sinful Folly's nod,
Forbear to sing of righteousness and God ?

A nobler task be mine. To wake within
  The dreaming soul a higher view
Of life's mysterious worth ; and thoughts of sin
  And wrong, not falsely, fatally untrue :
To sing of liberty for hearts oppress'd,
And promises of true, abiding rest.

To go where pining sorrow's burden weighs,
  With crushing weight, on lone afflicted hearts,
And there to sing such simple, tender lays,
  As the inspiring Soul, Himself imparts,—
Softly, as dews o'er fainting flowrets steal,
Soothing the sorrows which they cannot heal.

To hurl contempt on every guise of wrong,
  Tho' selfish thousands may proclaim it right ;
To raise the spirit chain'd to earth too long,
  And fire with earnest purpose, to unite
With all the brave and good of mortal race,
In making earth a holier, happier place.

To celebrate, in thankful, truthful numbers,
Nature's rare grandeur, beauty and delight,

The morning's glory, breaking nightly slumbers,—
    The dreamy musings of the starry Night,—
The lights and shadows of the world within,—
The joy of faith and wretchedness of sin.

Though fools may sneer, immortal man is not
    The fleeting creature of a fleeting day,
That life's high destiny should be forgot,
    And its rare pearls all madly flung away,
Far deeper wants his thirsting spirit feels,
And loftier purpose to his soul appeals.

Strong, stifled yearnings of celestial birth,
    In calmer hours, beat in his bosom's deep,
Stealing the charm from all the joys of earth,
    Where cares perplex and blighting tempests sweep;
Like some lone child whom fate compels to roam,
When darkness lowers he breathes a wish for home.

Let not the soulless cynic falsely say,
    "The age of poetry and love is o'er."
Nature reveals no symptoms of decay;
    She is not now less beauteous than of yore;
The themes, which charm the Poet while he sings,
Are streams that flow from never-failing springs.

The sleepless ocean is as wild and vast,
    As when its dirge first broke on mortal ears;
The starry heavens, thro' all the ages past,
    Could boast no splendors, lost to later years:

Spring's buds and blossoms still are fresh and fair;
And Autumn's gifts are ever rich and rare.

The heart is deep as ever in its swell;
    Youth yields its joy, and faith its strength imparts;
Truth, love, and beauty have not lost their spell;
    The blood still bounds at deeds of hero hearts:
Music still soothes the spirit crush'd with grief;
And tender sympathy brings sweet relief.

And though no errant knight on prancing steed
    Goes forth, in tested armor clad, to spoil
Some giant foe, and rescue maid in need,
    Yet heroes live, whose selfdenying toil;—
Unsung by fame, to hearts with anguish riven
Conveys the light of hope, and balm of heaven.

To all to whom the lays of life are dear,
    I now commit these rustic, broken strains :
If they should dry a fellow-mourner's tear,—
    A moment soothe a burden'd sufferer's pains,—
Wake torpid hearts to thoughts unfelt before,
Or guide a soul toward heaven—I ask no more.

THE POET'S MISSION.

A S one, who watches, from the surf-worn beach,
A vessel freighted with his hoarded wealth,
Spreading her canvas for some distant port,
Far o'er the faithless, melancholy main,
Shrouds in his breast conflicting hopes and fears,
Such thoughts are mine, launching my little book,
Freighted with musings of my pensive hours,
From the calm haven of its natal heart,
To breast the tide-waves of the living deep.

I know not whether favoring winds shall waft
It safe, into the haven of a sunny fame ;
Or harsher gales of scorn, and cold neglect,
Long ere it gain that distant shore, shall doom
To fill some dim and nameless resting-place,
In the chaotic gulfs of dark oblivion ;
Within whose rayless depths, unhonored, sleep
Thousands, who once have dreamed of fadeless bays.

Many there be who scorn the Poet's lays,
As dreamings of a fevered brain ; who know

No higher good than sordid gain bestows,—
No purer joy than selfish longings slaked;
To whom the beauty, harmony, and power,
Inscribed on mountain, vale, and sapphire sea,
In characters of love, by Him who gifts
The bard with skill to read His glorious thoughts,
Are all a sealed unmeaning book, obscured
By shallow, brainless thoughts of truth and life :
Made in His image, yet forever blind
To shining footprints of a present God ;
And deaf to symphonies divinely grand,
Which thrill with rapture every quicken'd ear.
The grandest poetry, that stirs the soul,
Is traced by His unseen and potent hand,
Who hung the heavens with lamps of living light,
And vested earth in wild and wondrous beauty.
And though the sordid heart may grovel in
Congenial spheres of thought, well-pleased with low
Pursuits, yet as we rise in purity,—
In love of truth and goodness, visions grand,
That swell the poet's soul with speechless joy,—
Though words not half reveal what he has felt,—
Shall, more and more, have power to kindle thoughts,
Which lift us on their wings of flame toward heaven.

Under the burden of bewildering cares,
Which fate has laid on every child of earth,
We need the charm of Fancy's gentle strains

To lull our fretful feverish thoughts to sleep ;
And lift awhile above this leaden world,
Whose ceaseless strife encrusts the heart, and scars
The gentler sympathies that sweeten life.

As Science to our wondering gaze reveals
The hidden forces of the universe,
So Poesie unveils the earthly types
Of things divine.   When shadows shroud the life,
She opes to sight the golden orbs of heaven ;
And pours upon the jarr'd and weary heart
Glad lays of hope and joy ; which, like the harp
Of Jesse's son, drive back to their infernal home
Spirits of envy, hate, distrust, and pride.
But he whose ear is closed against the voice
Of poetry, the music of the soul,
Shuts out the healing sunshine from his thoughts,
And lives immured in selfish gloom, which sours
His heart, and mantles life with sullen skies.

Scorn not the Poet, lest thy blindness scorn
Him also, who hath touched his soul with fire.
He digs the diamonds from the mines of thought,
And brings rare pearls from truth's vast ocean deeps.
His touch translates the slave of grimy toil
And poverty, into a fairy land,
Where fields are always green, and rivers flow

In silvery radiance, free from icy bonds,
And stars forever shine in cloudless joy.
In such release from life's dull drudgery,
He gathers images of beauty, peace,
And love, whose light shall beam on darker hours ;
And strength to travel on his craggy way
With lighter step, and fight life's battles with
A braver heart. A priest, by Heaven ordained,
The Poet-seer at Nature's altar stands
To offer reverent worship for his race ;
To coin in burning language golden truths,
Bodied in nature's hieroglyphic forms ;
And word the grateful joy, and trusting love
And hope, which thousands feel but cannot speak.

Go stand upon some towering height, from which
The eye can sweep o'er wide extended scenes
Of beauty, grandeur, and delight, outspread
By bounteous Nature with maternal pride.
Gaze upon lakes and rivers, beautiful
And bright, like molten silver flashing in
The Summer's sun.—On fields that wave with rich
Rewards for honest toil, while grateful winds
Are freighted with the balmy breath of flowers ;—
And song of birds, and sound of piping streams,
And zephyrs breathing musically low,
Harmonious speak the universal joy.
Look on the ocean in its chainless might

And dark and treach'rous beauty, scorning time :
Survey the golden orbs that crown the Night.
Behold the peerless tints of Autumn woods,
And all the changing splendors of the year.
Search well that vaster world, the human mind ;
With all its ocean deeps and prairies wide,—
Its moods of wintry storm and summer peace,—
Its nights of darkness, agony and tears,—
Its days of golden light and gushing joy,—
Its mystic powers and deathless thoughts, which speak,
In words of light, of parentage divine.
Then, as thy bosom swells with sacred joy,
That vainly yearns to mould itself in speech,
Rejoice, that God in tenderness has given,
To earth-born bard, the power to voice in words
The joy, sublimity, and tenderness,
These works divine have kindled in his breast.

In lays, by beauty, purity, and truth,
Inspired, each child of toil may see with joy
The visions which he saw ; may hear the strains
Of sweet unworded harmony he heard ;
Until the torpid spirit wakes, to feel
The conscious pulses of a higher life.

SONG OF THE WIND.

E spirits of air, so potent and fair,
   That roam through the starry sky,
  Follow my flight on your pinions light,
   For who is more mighty than I?
  Like you I sweep, through the liquid deep,
   Invisible, swift, and strong,
And gladness or woe dispense as I go,
  With gentle or terrible song.

Through the night I sleep, in the cloudy deep,
  That hangs o'er the sleeping Earth,
Which darkens the gleams of the starry beams,
  And gives the fierce lightnings birth.
I awake ere the Sun has his race begun,
  When the East glows with crimson and gold—
I stir the trees, with a gentle breeze,
  And dance o'er the misty wold.

When the scorching blaze, of the Summer's rays,
  Its burdensome langour brings,
I silently fan both beast and man
  With my cool invisible wings.

I carry the rain from the distant main,
  Like a patient servant of toil,
And fling it in showers o'er the drooping flowers,
  And the sunburnt thirsty soil.

To the fevered cheek of the faint and weak
  A grateful balm I impart;
And in sultry hours, with the breath of flowers,
  I gladden the weary heart.
When the earth is cold, and the Winter grows old,
  I bring the warm breath of Spring,
And my power is felt, when the ice-chains melt,
  And the rivers in concert sing.

I breathe through the trees, a musical breeze,—
  On my wind-harp the forest I play;
When I pass in the storm wearing terror's form,
  Then the forest-kings bow to my sway.
I rend the oak, with the whirlwind's stroke,
  Or play with the thistle-down;
When I sink to sleep, the blue heavens weep,
  And the silver dew comes down.

When the heavens are dark, and each golden spark
  Is mantled from mortal view,
I scatter the clouds, those starry shrouds,
  And open the boundless blue.
With favouring gales, I fill the sails
  Of the vessels that plough the main,

Till the sailors rejoice, with merry voice,
    When they reach the haven again.

From the mountain height, in the depths of night,
    I swiftly and silently launch
On its perilous leap from the rocky steep,
    The death-dealing avalanche.
When I playfully flow into caverns below,
    Far down into the fire-hearted earth,
Then the spirits, who dwell in each stygian cell,
    Rejoice at an earthquake's birth.

I strip the leaves from the forest trees,
    And scatter them far and wide,
Till they spangle the plain with colour and stain,
    As fair as in Summer's pride.
I madly blow the fresh-fallen snow,
    And pile it in glittering heaps,
Till the hillocks rise, to Fancy's eyes,
    Like the grave where a giant sleeps.

When I sink to rest, on the Earth's broad breast,
    Into mute tranquil air I flow;
On my noiseless wing, I ceaselessly bring
    The echoes of joy and woe.
The secrets I hide, in my chambers wide,
    Fill mortals with awe and wonder:
On the lightning's glance I merrily dance,
    And I laugh at the pealing thunder.

O'er the mountains high, which are lost in the sky,
I skip with an airy tread;
But the midnight hour is the time of my power.
  When the snowy carpet is spread:
Then, in doleful shrieks the night-wind speaks,
  To summon the demons of air;
And there seems a strife, as for death and life,
  Which is followed by groans of despair.

When the ocean vast hears my trumpet blast
  Roll over its bosom wide,
Then up from the deep the billows leap,
  In their fierce untameable pride :
On the rocky shore, their sullen roar
  Fills the mariner's home with dread ;
For their comes a wail upon every gale,
  As sad as the voice of the dead—
A passionate moan, full of anguish and lone,
  The cry of the Spirit of ocean,
Wildly pleading, to move the heavens above
  To tender and ruthful emotion.

When I sweep in wrath on my briny path,
  The vessels my might who brave,
With their precious freight, yield to merciless fate,
  And are buried beneath the wave.
And they weep on the land, the deeds of my hand,
  In many a sorrowful dwelling ;
But my stern heart can know nought of pity for woe,
  When the tide of my ire is swelling.

Over land, over sea, still tireless I flee,
  Like my guardian spirit the Sun,
The day may go, and the night may flow,
  My labour is never done.
Neither sun nor rain, which ripen the grain,
  Bring gifts more precious and rare ;
For life and health are the priceless wealth,
  That are brought by the winds of air.

None of mortal birth—no monarch of earth—
  Has an empire so grand and wide ;
Since the birth of Time, over every clime
  I have swayed my sceptre with pride.
And yet, though I sing with the pride of a king,
  And boast of my boundless sway,
His servant am I, Who ruleth on high,
  Whom the winds and the seas obey.

VOICES OF THE PAST.

THE last faint gleam of Evening's golden light
 Has softly died away. With noiseless hand,
 The Autumn twilight-shades enshroud from sight
   Both sea and land.

In the hushed stillness of the darkened air,
Like lonely echoes of the surging main,
The Voices of the Past, with music rare,
   Float through my brain.

Their mournful tones enchant my listening ears
Like spirit songs. The throng my soul unsought,
Rich with the hoarded gold of vanished years,
   And pearls of thought.

Like winds and waves, that swift and viewless sweep,
Freighted with treasures from some far-off clime,
They bare rich argosies across the deep,
   Dark sea of Time.

They speak of courtly pomp, and regal power
And fame, which now in dark oblivion lie;
Of queenly beauty, fair as fairest flower,
   Which bloomed to die.

Of battles fought and bloody victories won,
For selfish lust of power, and hollow fame—
Of falsehood, tyranny, and crimes which none
  Can calmly name.

Of love as changeless as the stars of heaven—
Of joy that flashed—like lightning on the deep—
And left the soul, in rayless tempests driven,
  To watch and weep.

Of sunless paths, where Doubt and Darkness lower—
Of Superstition's black and ruthless reign—
Of hero-faith, which gave the god-like power
  To smile at pain.

Of Morn, unveiling truths long vainly sought,
Beaming refulgent o'er the weary night
Of years—gilding the hills and vales of thought
  With holy light.

Of Freedom battling with immortal might—
Baffled and crushed in vain—victorious still—
Of Kingly hearts, who still maintained the right
  With iron will.

Of Poet-souls, whose grand immortal lays
Still float o'er fallen thrones and royal names—
And some, who sang in sorrow all their days,
  Oblivion claims.

Of ardent minds, whose fruitless years were spent
Yearning for light, for truth, and spirit rest ;
But sought them not of God, and died at length,
    Sad and unblest.

From thy dark bosom unrelenting Past,
These whispers of the buried years are borne—
Mysterious moonless sea, though deep and vast.
    Lifeless and lorn !

No stormy winds disturb thy waveless breast—
No starry skies dispel thine ebon gloom—
All beauteous things, whose light and love have blest,
    There find a tomb.

Life, like a river from the Future, sweeps
Along its shores with melody sublime,
Bearing forever to those silent deeps
    The wrecks of Time.

The wrecks of ardent love, of power and pride—
Of Hope, that vainly battled with Despair—
Of life, that sparkled like a mountain tide,
    Lie buried there.

Mysterious, grand, and melancholy Past !
Empire of Death, Oblivion, and Decay !
Darkness shall veil thy depths, until the last
    Great Judgment-day.

Till then, thou holdest in thine iron hand
Records, by which immortal fate is given—
Deeds that shall rise and shine at God's command,
    As stars of heaven.

Weird ghostly messengers, your words remind
Of blighted blossoms of my wasted years—
Of broken vows and baffled hopes, which blind
    With bitter tears.

Ye thrill—with memories of forgotten pleasure,—
Becloud with shadows of forgotten sadness,
And strangely blend in one harmonious measure,
    Both grief and gladness.

And yet, each whispered note of dirge-like tone
My sad and faithless heart with hope inspires,
For brighter burns, as Time has onward flown,
    Truth's beacon-fires.

Ye bid the doubting spirit trust and wait,—
Remind that fruits most precious ripen slowly,—
That love and goodness only make us great,
    And raise the lowly.

Earth's brightest joy-stars fade and are forgot,
But all that Heaven's immortal founts supply—
Truth, holy love, kind deeds, and noble thought
    Shall never die.

BARTIMEUS.

Waif upon the troubled stream of time,
Drifted and tossed about by fickle Fate,
He lived a lone and sorrow-stricken life;
Shut out from nature's beauty, light and joy,
Bereft of all that could assuage his woes,
Or smooth his rough and joyless way. None know
So well the selfishness of human hearts,
As those whom stern misfortune has ordained
To test their sympathy.

                    The only star
That shed a gleam of solace on his gloom,
The one bright oasis, that still kept green
In the bleak desert of his flowerless life,
With nought to break its dull monotony,
Was the remembrance of a mother's love.
Her loving words,—the psalms she sweetly sang,—
Her tender kisses on his infant lips,—
These were the golden memories of his life.
Like some rare jewels kept in poverty,
As sad remembrancers of happier times,
Deep in the sacred chambers of his heart
He kept them safe to light his lonely hours;

And, though he scarcely knew what beauty meant.
He thought that one, whose touch was gentleness.
With tones so soft, and heart so warm and true.
Must sure have been to sight most beautiful.
She died ere childhood blossomed into youth,
And left him friendless, destitute and blind.
Of his dead father memory kept no trace.

'Tis Summer morn: the vivifying dews
Of night the sun has long exhaled: the hills
And vales are robed in deepest emerald,
Besprent with beauteous flowers: all nature smiles;
But the fair scene gives not a single gleam
Of sunshine to the beggar's weary heart;
Whose sightless eyes had never read the signs
By which the living world reveals its joy.
He sits a-begging by the highway side,
In lone despondency; and sick at heart,
That Heaven had made it his unpitied lot
To be both poor and blind.

             The scorching sun
Scatters his burning rays, with fierce delight,
Upon the naked hills; and he is driven,
At length, to seek the cool and kindly shade
Of the wide-branching sycamore, which, with
A touch akin to human sympathy,
Spread its long arms to shield his throbbing head.

It is a sad and unpropitious day

With Bartimeus, for the tiny spring,
At which so long he daily quenched his thirst,
Had dried; and though 'tis past the noon, and men
Have passed along the way since early morn,
Not one has paused to hear his tale of grief,
Or pity his distress. Pensive and lone
He sits; nerving at times his sinking heart
By whispered words of prayer to Jacob's God,
The faithful Friend and Helper of the poor.
But when he thought on the unbroken night,
In which his life was spent, in bitterness
Of soul he pray'd, that he might die, and be
At rest forever from the want and scorn,
Which Fate had mingled with his cup of life.

At length, attracted by the shady tree,
A traveller from Jericho drew near,
And with the beggar shared his homely meal.
And more, he spoke him kindly words, which fell
Like soothing music on his bleeding heart.
He told him of a prophet, great and good,
Who had appeared among Judea's hills;
By whom the lame were healed, the lepers cleansed,
The blind received their sight; and even the dead
Called back from hades at his sovereign word:
And best of all, the poor and lowly ones,
Whom Pharisees and Scribes contemned with scorn,
Received his ready aid and kind regard.
With rapt attention Bartimeus heard
The wondrous tale; while joy, and doubt, and hope,

And wonder swept across his face ;
And from his sightless eyes rolled grateful tears,
Which with his ragged cloak he wiped away :
For he remembered, while the stranger spoke,
Such were the deeds of grace his mother told
The holy prophets wrote the Christ would do.
He was afraid to hope, lest hope should prove
A faithless snare ; yet fervently he prayed
That God might send this holy prophet near.
But, when his transient guest had gone his way,
And left him to his lonely thoughts again,
At times, he fancied all was but a dream,
A flash of hope across an ocean of despair.

At length the waning heat signals the day's
Decline ; the touch of fairy-fingered Eve
Has bathed the world in mellow, golden light,
In which all things look glad and beautiful.
Deeming it vain to tarry longer, he
Prepared to seek the hovel where he dwelt;
But, as he rises to depart, his ear
Catches the hum as of a multitude,
Like the low murmur of a coming storm.
He cannot tell its cause.   His heart beats loud
And fast.   There may be danger in his path.
Nearer the tumult comes.   He cannot flee :
Though sounds of angry strife at hand he hears.
Eager he calls aloud ; but none reply.
At last one near him answered, as in wrath,

" *'Tis Jesus, Nazareth's healing prophet come.*"
A thrill of hope shot through the blind man's soul.
He thought this hour might be his only hope ;
It might be God had heard his lowly prayer :
And, with a strong and pleading voice, he cried,
Jesus, thou son of David, pity me.
And, as he called aloud, some near him, vex'd
By his continued cries, rebuked his zeal,
And sharply bid him hush his brawling tongue ;
And asked him, if he thought the prophet had
No more to do than wait on one like him ?
For in their Pharisaic thoughts, they deemed
A man might be reputed great and good,
Yet close his ears against the cry of grief.
But, still, he only cried the more, as if
The stiffled agony of his dark life
Of friendless woe, at last had found a tongue.

Then He, whose ear is ever open to
The sufferer's cry, attracted by his calls,
Told those around to bring the blind man near.
Officious voices pass'd the word along ;
And Bartimeus, with a beating heart,
Catching the word that *he* was called, arose
And, flinging off his tattered cloak in haste,
Bounded away from those who led him, till,
As if by some unerring instinct led,
He cast himself at Jesus' feet, and cried
Aloud, *Thou Son of David pity me.*

The Master took him by the hand, bade him
Arise, and asked what boon from him he craved?
His ready answer came without delay,—
Lord I am blind, to me my sight restore.
Then Jesus said, *be it according to*
Thy faith; and instantly, his rayless night
Of years was turned to bright and blessed day.

Bewildered, for a moment, there he stood,
Entranced in speechless wonder and delight,
With all the glory of the sunset hour
Flushing his radiant, wonder-stricken face:
Then fixed his glance with grateful love upon
The face, where wisdom, truth, and tenderness
Divine, with purity and peace were blent;
And then, with words of grateful praise upon
His lips, he followed Jesus in the way.

THE UNSPOKEN.

BENEATH the heedless, wandering feet,
  Deep mines of precious ore may lie.
Below the icy plain, how fleet
  The mighty river rushes by!
So 'neath the calm of outer life,
  The tides of thought and feeling roll:
There, in the deep unwritten strife,
  Is wrought the history of the soul.

Hid in the vast primeval wood,
  Under its shades of leafy green,
Are lone retreats, where never stood
  A human foot, where all unseen
By mortal eye comes Summer's bloom,
  And Autumn's glory fades away,
And Winter buries in his tomb
  The beauteous emblems of decay.

So in the twilight of the soul
  Is many a dim and hidden place,
Where sad eolián murmurs roll,
  And Pain its autograph doth trace;
To which the friends of kindliest heart,
  For sympathy by nature fitted,

Though true, and free from guileful art,
   Through life have never been admitted.

The shallow heart by passion swept,
   Whose life is all an idle song,
Who never hath in secret wept
   O'er strangled hopes and selfish wrong,
May have no hidden, voiceless dream,—
   No wounds concealed from friendship's sight,—
May, like a clear and pebbly stream,
   Spread all its treasures to the light :
But every earnest, thoughtful mind,
   At times in lonely paths has trod,—
Felt wordless grief, and joy refined,
   And thoughts unknown to all but God.

As in the busy crowd, we feel
   A sense of loneliness, as deep
As if on some deserted isle
   By Fate ordained to watch and weep,
So, 'mid the throng of common cares,
   There comes a tender lonely thought,
Which some mysterious token bars,
   And never into words is wrought.

It may be when the friend of years,
   To whom our trustful love was given,
Like ship that from its pathway veers,
   By adverse currents wildly driven,

By some unholy influence swept,
  Betrays the confidence of youth,
Faithless and false as guile's adept,
  And wounds our faith in human truth.

Or else in sorrow's deadly blight,
  That withers life's most cherished flowers,
That quenches every starry light,
  Until the trembling spirit cowers
In dumb, despairing anguish keen,
  And feels, not words of seraph lips,
Can speak the agony unseen,
  That wrings the soul in Hope's eclipse.

Or when our dreams are bright and grand,
  As sunset palaces of air,
Or visions of some golden land,
  That never feels the breath of care.
When the rapt soul a glimpse has caught
  Of some achievement big with fame,
We fear to breathe the new-born thought,
  Lest fools should mock our cherished aim;
We hide it like the miser's gold,
  At which he only looks by stealth,
And sternly keeps till death untold
  The mildewed secret of his wealth.

It may be when the sun of love
  Dawns on the life, serenely bright,

And earth below and heaven above
  Are tinted with the rosy light:
When softly flow the silvery rills
  Of joy, to lull all jarring care;
And sombre rocks and naked hills
  Robes of refulgent beauty wear.

Then swells a gladness, deep and rare,—
  So full of tender, guiltless shame,
We scarce can think it true, or dare
  To link with ours the cherished name;
But like a child, who softly steals
  To watch a wood-bird's secret nest,
With bashful silence each conceals
  The joy that trembles in his breast.

Or who could dare to trust his tongue
  With what his burdened spirit feels,
When all to which his faith has clung,
  As firm and true, totters and reels;
And mind, and truth, and being crowd
  Their mighty problems on his brain,
Till vainly toiling to unshroud
  The truth, his joy is turned to pain.

When Doubt has covered with her veil
  The guiding way-marks of the heart,
His chainless thoughts in silence sail
  O'er seas, not traced on human chart,—

Of friendly sympathy bereft,
   The lonely strife no mortal sees,—
Companions of the past are left
   Behind, on more pacific seas.
Or worse—a leak his vessel springs—
   He never gains the port he sought—
To some frail plank he wildly clings,
   Swept by the restless waves of thought—
And if the land at length be gained,
   And safe on shore his limbs repose,
All that he felt, while Doubt maintained
   Dark sway, he never can disclose.

Or who in words can fitly shrine
   The guilt, the anguish, and despair,
When conscience, like a voice divine,
   Lays all our deeds of darkness bare:
When, at the voiceless midnight hour,
   We trace the path our feet have trod;
And, touched with solemn mystic power,
   The soul is face to face with God?

The battles with temptation fought—
   The scorn by pride and envy cast—
The joy and pain of lonely thought—
   The tender memories of the past—
The baffled hopes—the hidden care—
   The griefs that never found a tongue,
Are thrilling epics, rich and rare,
   Which mortal bard has never sung.

T was a sombre autumn day;
   The sky with leaden clouds was hung:
   The winds, with weird and restless tongue,
  Were piping many a mournful lay.

With spirit chafed with care, and pained,
   I wandered through an ancient wood,
   And long, in dark desponding mood,
Of all created things complained.

"And why," I asked, "has man been made
   The victim of unending sorrow?
   Hope paints a joy to come to-morrow—
To-morrow comes to see it fade.

If sin is followed by a train
   Of scorpion stings, and nameless woes,
   That at the heels of Error goes,
Bound fast by Fate's eternal chain,

Then why are there to mortals given
   Those burnings of unhallowed fires,
   This eager thirst of wrong desires,
Which lead the soul away from heaven?

Our life is like a sunless cave,
  Whose trait'rous murkiness conceals
  The pits and chasms, light reveals,
When light has come too late to save.

The world is full of pits ; the lights
  And way-marks vainly sought ;
  And men of deepest, keenest thought,
But dream through darker nights.

Each seems a guideless pilgrim, who
  Through moonless life a journey takes,
  And knows not, when the morning breaks,
What scenes shall burst upon his view.

And why are cold and selfish hearts,
  Strangers to nobleness and love,
  Unblest by thoughts of God above,
Or hopes which holy faith imparts,

The rich possessors of the soil,
  Sheltered from every storm that blows,
  While aching Want's unnumbered woes
Oppress the honest sons of toil ?

Blossoms of hope, before life's prime,
  Death strikes with swift and fatal aim :
Extinguished like a taper's flame,
  They leave the world before their time.

While those whose lives are pain and tears—
  Or worse, whose blighted, tainted mind
  Is but a curse to all their kind,
Live on through lengthened, weary years.

The path of life has many a thorn,
  And much is dark that needs be clear;
  Of truth we know but little here,
And scarce see why we have been born.

Do angels watch unseen, tho' nigh,
  For good and evil while we stay?
  And where, when sleeps the mortal clay,
Does the undying spirit fly?

There is no joy unmixed with grief,—
  Each garden has more weeds than flowers,—
  Care rides upon the wingèd hours,
And doubt forever haunts belief.

We bend to drink of some bright rill,
  Whose cooling waters laughing glide,
  And find it is a poisoned tide—
Promise and hope with failure fill.

We stop to pluck some beauteous flower,
  And cold precaution idly scorn,
  To find some sharp and hidden thorn,
Exacts a forfeit for the dower.

There have been tears of wormwood shed,
   For every pleasure life can bring;
   The joys of earth are flowers that spring
From out the ashes of the dead."

Long thus I spoke; I scarce knew why—
   My thoughts seem'd broken from control;
   Awhile I ceased; and thus my soul,
To my dark thoughts made soft reply.

" Not all in vain do sorrows here
   Pierce with keen arrows every heart;
   Lessons divine their lips impart:
There's balm and blessing in a tear.

The griefs, which every heart must know,
   Which earth is powerless to console,
   May keep the tendrils of the soul
From taking deeper root below.

The storm that sways the forest trees,
   Still roots them deeper in the soil;
   So sorrow, conflict, care, and toil
Nurture our strength by slow degrees.

If deeds which men heroic name,
   No self-denying will required,
   And every heart the right desired,
What praise could acts of virtue claim?

Those mysteries, to thought obscure,
　　May test and strengthen trusting love :
　　But why should what is hidden move
Our faith in what we know is sure?

The prompting cause of many a deed,
　　The parent from the child conceals ;
　　But, long as life true love reveals,
Why should distrust to darkness lead ?

What Heaven has not been pleased to show,—
　　What mortal vision cannot see—
　　If Heaven is wise, it cannot be
That this were best for us to know.

Our Father, infinitely wise,
　　Through time evolves a boundless scheme,
　　We see a part, and falsely dream
That all is spread before our eyes.

What though this world present to sight,
　　Confusion, mystery, and gloom,
　　In the pure world beyond the tomb,
We yet shall see that all was right.

A thousand causes round us yield
　　Results, we never would have thought
　　Could from such origin be brought,
If life had not the truth revealed.

Though ruthless seems the Winter wild,
  The Spring is sleeping in its breast;
  And snow-storms braid her flowery vest;
For genial Spring is Winter's child.

Though, like a ship, our life appears,
  Careering o'er the midnight deep,
  We know while all around may sleep,
Unslumb'ring Heaven our vessel steers.

Too often, with perverted eye,
  We look on what is dark alone;
  And never see, around us strewn,
Tokens of love that cannot die.

What ample stores this orb reveals,
  Thro' ages hid from mortal ken,
  To satisfy the wants of men,
And show the care our Father feels.

Nor aught less freely has he given
  Supplies for spirit-want and woe,
  Streams in the desert softly flow;—
Through clouds we catch a glimpse of heaven.

Tho' weak to vanquish mighty ills,
  He gives the fainting spirit might,—
  Pierces our darkness with heaven's light,
And on our griefs his peace distills.

The weakness and the want, which twine
  Our being in their mazy folds,
  Come not because His hand withholds,
But from our slight of gifts divine.

Wait not, in idleness and sin,
  All truth and knowledge sought to gain;
  The darkest problems of the brain
Grow brighter when there's light within.

Not he who doubts and dreams thro' life,
  But he who toils in faith below,
  The mystery of life shall know,
And harmony discern in strife.

THE WINTER OF LIFE.

THE worlds that stud the cope of heaven display
Tokens of undecaying youth. The sun,
Whose beams for ages past have fill'd the vast
Immensity of space with light, still burns
With undimished blaze. The golden stars—
Unwaning beacons in a shoreless sea—
Untarnished by the lapse of fateful years,
Sparkle as brilliantly, as when at first
Projected on their circling paths of light,
Fresh from the hand of God. But here, decay
And change are the predestined fate of all
That blooms to beautify and gladden earth.
There is no blessed shore, no island in
The sea, no deep retreat, no sheltered glen,
Where comes not the chill blighting breath of Fate.
The footsteps of the silent Years deface
And crush life's rarest plants. The monuments
Of human power are lost in Time's dark deeps.

But chiefly is the sceptre of decay,
Over the realms of beauty, swayed with stern
Destructive might. The fairest forms of earth,
That nestle in the love of kindly hearts,
Are first to perish 'neath the tread of Time.

The queenliest flower of all, whose beauty seems
The mystic growth of some celestial seed,
Borne on the zephyr's wings, from that far clime
Where golden stars, like flowers unfading, bloom
In the broad gardens of the sky, is first
To droop aud mingle with its native clay.
The kingliest tree, that stands in stalwart pride,
And spreads its foliage to the Summer's sun,
Shall fall at length, before the wintry blast.
The brightest visions Hope and Fancy paint
On the broad canvass of the coming years,
Like sun-set glories, herald shades of night.
Life has its spring, when every breeze that blows
Breathes hope and gladness through the bounding heart;
And those who sow the seeds of righteousness
Shall reap the precious fruits of peace at last.
But swiftly comes the season of decline,
When fairest types of mortal strength and beauty
Shall feel the touch of age, disease, and pain;
And droop in cureless weakness and decay—
Chill wintry hours, when the green Summer leaves,
And crimson blossoms of the spring dissolve
In dust, beneath the ruthless snows of age.

How desolate his poverty of soul,
Who has been sailing towards that silent shore,
Whose shades the gleams of earthly hope cannot
Dispel, with selfish Folly at the helm !
Who, when the shadows of old age have wrapt
In darkness all the stars of life, has in

His soul no joy of faith to light its gloom.
If all is dark without, O doubly dark
And drear is he, who has no light within!
The active limbs no longer fleetly roam
O'er hills and vales, with buoyant, joyous tread;
The failing eyes no more with rapture gaze
On beauteous scenes which Nature's hand unveils;
The leaden ear no longer drinks the sound
Of melody and love. The faithful hearts
Whose friendship was the dew of dawning life—
The sunlight of departed years of joy—
Are far away, or pulseless in the grave.
Perchance ingratitude, or cold neglect,
Combine with memories of baffled dreams,
To add their gall-drops to the bitter cup,
Which now in weakness and decay he drains.
The body bows beneath infirmity and pain;
The mind grows dull, and, like an eagle of
His pinions reft, sweeps o'er the fields of thought
No more. The joy of mingling in life's whirl
Is gone. A bridgeless gulf now gapes between
Him and the halcyon days of hopeful toil.

In such an hour, shut out from active labour,
The soul turns inward, preying on itself,
And on the dark irrevocable past,
Whose spectral memories haunt life's twilight hour:
And like a dying hemlock there he stands
Awhile, in leafless solitary blight,
Till the last rotten root refuse to bind

Him longer to his native earth. The springs
Of youthful joy, like streams that dry beneath
The Summer's ardent blaze, yield no supply
When needed most. The lamps that lit his way
Go out as night and darkness gather round.

Or if he wear the semblance of repose,
And outer calm betokens peace within,
'Tis but the listless stupor of a soul
Unconscious of its dignity and fate ;
Immured in living sepulchre, and dead
To all the grandeur of immortal life,
And all the dark unfathomed woes of sin.

If selfish passion has controlled the life,
And guilt uncancelled on the conscience weighs,
As evening shadows fall, where can true hope
Or peace be found by him, who has through all
Life's years shut out his Maker from his heart ?
His backward glance surveys, with vain regret,
The joyless memories of the vanished Past,
Peopled with phantoms of remorse and sin.
Or if some brighter spots to thought arise,
Like gleams of sunshine o'er the wasted years,
They, too, were sacrificed to sordid self,
And like rich pearls, whose worth was all unknown,
Were madly flung away. Or if he look
Within, his soul is dark and desolate ;
And from the future every thought recoils,
As from a region in whose bosom hides

Despair, and unimaginable grief,
Which spread their shadows o'er the ebbing life,
Now flickering in its dark and joyless close.

A shipwrecked sailor on a desert isle—
A lonely barque without supplies or compass,
Launching upon a dark, uncharted sea—
A houseless wanderer on an Arctic shore—
A thirsty traveller over desert sands—
Is wintry age with piety unblest.
And he who trusts and loves the glittering things,
O'er which Corruption and Decay have power,
Prepares the soil, and sows the seed, whose fruit
Is Sorrow, Disappointment, and Despair.
For if the temple of our hope, in which
The soul seeks refuge and repose, give way,
The false and baseless dreams must perish too.
Yet those who waste the golden summer hours
In vain pursuit of pleasure, pelf, or power,
And leave the winter of their years without
Provision for its varied wants and woes,
Most keenly hunger for protracted life.

In the bright summer of our fleeting years,
When thick-robed trees extend their sheltering arms
To form a gorgeous canopy above,
When every breeze is redolent with flowers,
And sultry zephyrs of the sunny South
Lull into dreamy thoughtlessness and joy,
We seek no shelter, but the vault of heaven.

But ah! when Winter's unrelenting hand
Has left the trees in leafless nakedness,
When the keen air, by Nature's mystic power,
Appears transmuted into blistering flame,
And fierce unpitying storms are sweeping o'er
The naked hills, how merciless his fate,
Who knows no refuge from the strife of Nature,
In her dark moods of unrelenting ire.

But richly blest are they, who when old-age
Has scared the dewy blossoms of their youth,
And dried the fountains of remembered joys,
By faith, with joy, drink from the living stream,
That flows perennial from the throne of Love ;
And feel, as ligaments of flesh decay,
The pulse of life immortal stronger beat.
To such the memories of the past are full
Of grateful joys, and living faith in God reveals
Visions more beautiful and grand, than all
The wasted glories of the bygone years.
While all the lights of Earth grow dim and fail,
The light which Heaven has kindled in the heart,
By Heaven sustained, burns with undying flame—
Brightens the weary solitude of Age,
And scatters all the shadows of the tomb.

A NOBLEMAN'S GRAVE.

THE day is softly fading into night;
 The forest trees wear Autumn's brilliant dyes;
The glassy stream, in floods of golden light,
 Flings back the glory of the western skies.

From the deep shadows of her lone retreat,
 While all the forest choristers are still,
Float through the listening twilight, wild and sweet,
 The mournful vespers of the Whip-poor-will.

Here, in the melancholy twilight gray,
 Among the dead, I seek a lowly tomb,—
With pensive joy, a willing tribute pay
 To one, for whom no earthly laurels bloom.

This rude, unlettered stone points out the place,
 Where in obscurity, forgotten sleeps
A patient son of toil, whose honest race
 And hero deeds no mortal record keeps.

No truer worth could friendship's tribute claim,—
 No kindlier memories throng my heaving breast,
If musing over tombs embalmed by Fame,
 Where Poets, Kings, and Conquerors rest.

In youth he gathered flowers on Erin's hills,
  And wondered at her tales of faëry lore :
He came, when Hope with fairest visions thrills,
  To seek a home on blue Ontario's shore.

Through weary years he struggled hard with fate,—
  Of ease or luxury he nothing knew :
He envied not the fortune of the great,
  Assured that Heaven is ever just and true.

He proved the joy of pure and trusting love,
  With one whose faith and kindness never failed ;
In darkest hours she bade him look above,
  And cheered with love, when Doubt and Fear assailed.

They drank of Sorrow's dark and bitter cup,—
  Earth has no blest retreats, where grief and pain
Fling not their shadows o'er the light of hope,
  To cloud the hopeful visions of the brain.

Beneath the forest trees they laid to rest
  A blue-eyed boy, unutterably dear,
Whose voice was rarest music, and whose love
  Was light and joy, when Fate was most severe.

Their lowly dwelling in the forest wild,
  By faith and love was bless'd and brighten'd still ;
In darkest hours Hope cheered her trusting child,
  And lent new vigor to his earnest will.

In wealth and poverty, the common tides
　Of human feeling flow through every heart.
The lowliest spirit in its history hides
　Life's purest joy, and sorrow's keenest smart.

He lived and died without applause or fame,
　Yet was his life heroic and sublime ;
Unsleeping Heaven has marked his lowly name
　And deeds among the fadeless stars of time.

No warrior brave, with guilt of blood to bear,
　He oft with enemies was sorely pressed,—
With Passion, Poverty, and grim Despair,
　Battles were fought and won within his breast.

Though all unschooled in philosophic lore,
　Alone with Nature in her forest fane,
Problems of life and truth were pondered o'er,
　And thoughts abstruse perplexed his busy brain.

And when his daily toil was o'er, he sought
　At night communion with the gifted dead,
Glancing along the starry paths of thought,
　Where only regal minds may dare to tread.

Ungifted he to sing of Nature's sheen,—
　No thoughts of beauty could his pen impart ;
Yet all that poets feel at times, I ween,
　Has throbb'd for utterance in his burning heart.

He could not solve, with argumental skill,
　　The subtle doubts of disbelief and pride,—
With simple faith he trusted God, and still
　　His word unfailing strength and light supplied.

No crouching slave to pride of wealth or birth,—
　　Not lordly airs could his stern will control;
He knew no standard of superior worth,
　　But wisdom, truth, and nobleness of soul.

His scorn of every selfish wrong was stern;
　　Yet kept his heart by human guile unsoured.
All human sorrow shared his deep concern,
　　And prompt his aid, when dark misfortune lower'd.

His life was earnest, manly, and sincere:
　　In death no faithless fears his soul betrayed.
Warm honest hearts, with many a gushing tear,
　　In this lone spot his mortal relics laid.

He too had faults, sincerely, sadly wept,—
　　Errors, whose memory gave him poignant pain;
Yet with a single heart his trust he kept,
　　And left a life untarnished by a stain.

A PLEA FOR LIBERTY.

T stirs the pulses of the blood
  With thrills of joy, to hear again
How lion-hearted heroes stood
  And fought, on many a gory plain,
For freedom in the olden days
  When stern oppression ruled the world;—
Or read, in warm impassioned lays,
  How tyrants from their thrones were hurl'd.

Or, when we hear of life-long slaves,
  By Freedom's touch transformed to men,
Though selfish prejudice still raves,
  We join humanity's "amen!"
We honor with our warm regard
  The martyrs who unshrinking died,
Rather than mortal man should lord
  Over the faith so sternly tried.

And shall we tamely wear a yoke,
  And slavish fetters on the mind,
Esteeming all some teacher spoke
  Or wrote, as gold refined?

Opinion, sentiment, or creed
   Which others firmly held and taught,
Cannot to us be truth indeed,
   Till it becomes our living thought.

When round the walls the foemen fight,
   New points to higher interest rise;
The truths, which once were lost to sight,
   May be the pearls which most we prize.
Each tome from ages past possest,
   Whatever guiding light it brings,
Is not a goal in which to rest,
   But steps to climb to higher things.

The falsehoods other ages fought,
   Perchance have vanished from the field,
And should we keep what truth they wrought
   Into their battle-axe and shield,
As if it were the whole complete,—
   All that the world can ever need,
And it were neither right nor meet
   To change or modify their creed.

The men, who fought in other days
   For free unshackled thought, we name
Immortal hero-souls, and raise
   The sculptured marble to their fame;
But strangely, living men like them,
   Who do not all our creed embrace,

With ruthless ardor we condemn,
  As heretics devoid of grace.

We follow best each kingly Saul,
  Who wrought and battled for the right,
And set the truths most dear to all,
  Through time in clearer, stronger light,—
Not by receiving all he taught,
  With faith unquestioning and blind,
But more, by seeking, as he sought,
  With fearless, independent mind.

As one who climbs some mountain height,
  That grandly lifts its peaks of snow,
Beholds, with wonder and, delight,
  Wide scenes, invisible below,
So through the gliding years of time,
  As suns revolve and earth grows old,
The snowy hills of thought we climb,
  And broader fields of truth behold.

As nature from the first possess'd
  Resources, long from mortals sealed,
Which seekers found within her breast,
  As Time by slow degrees revealed;
So does the Book of truth divine,
  To men from age to age unfold
New mines of thought and truth, which shine
  To faith, like stars of burnisht gold.

If we in science rise above
  Mistakes and errors of the past,
And only what is true approve,
  Where fancies long for truth have pass'd,
In fields of sacred thought, as well,
  We should reject the dross we meet,
Discern the kernel from the shell,
  And fan the chaff from out the wheat.

And if it be a crime, for me
  To search for Truth, with love sincere,
To follow where she leads me, free
  From doubting prejudice or fear,—
Even when my conscience bids me leave
  The path, which honored feet have trod,—
Then why, for what I here believe,
  Am I accountable to God?

In all the works of God we find
  A wondrous unity of thought;
Yet vast variety of kind
  With simple elements is wrought.
As different climes of earth produce
  Their different fruits of tree and field,
So gifts, condition, teaching, use,
  Diversity of thought must yield.

Shall I condemn, with stern disdain,
  The man who will not sign my creed;

Though he is with me in the main,
   And side by side in kindly deed?
If history's darkest page is traced
   In blood, by Christian bigots stern,
The war of creeds will never cease,
   Till charity from Christ we learn.

In thought, there must be false and true,—
   There must be wrong and right in deed;
Yet truth should value what we do,
   As highly as a lifeless creed.
The thoughts despised, as new or strange,
   May yet in regal triumph reign;—
The form and garb of truth may change,
   And yet the inner life remain.

AUTUMN EVENING.

’TIS evening’s holy hour. The sun has dipp’d
    Behind the hedge of maple, elm, and beech,
    That fringe the landscape on its western bourn ;
    A picture pencilled on a crimson sky.
    Here every harsh discordant sound is hush’d ;
    And soft tranquility broods over earth,
Lulling her fretful pulses into rest.
Nature has laid her finger on her lips,
And signal’d all her noisy votaries
To come not with unhallowed tread, to break
Upon her hour of deep and solemn worship.
Let me approach, with sympathetic heart,
And join in her unspoken prayer, and in
Th’ unworded hymn, that swells in noiseless praise
And love from her unsealed adoring lips.
In such an hour the echoes dissonant,
That fitly voiced the jarring passions of
The selfish heart, all blend and form a soft
Harmonious melody, which breathes repose,
Like a fond mother’s twilight cradle-song.

Unto my skyward glance, the vault of heaven
Seem vaster in its wide immensity,

Deeper than ever in its liquid blue;
And every sunlit cloud an airy palace,
Floating, all helmless, at its wayward will,
Thro' an illimitable sea, by storms
Unruffled, and by gloom undimm'd.
Yet have I seen thee, placid smiling Sky,—
Like beauty's face by selfish passion gloom'd,—
Darkened by murky clouds, obscured by fierce
And angry tempests, threatening direst woe,
Till Earth grew dark, and trembled at thy frown.

The lake is sleeping in the parting smile
Of the declining day. Its glassy breast
Mirrors unerringly the tranquil scenes,
That fringe it round, or canopy above.
A vast unfathomable deep it seems,
Grand in the borrowed glory of the sky.
Thus earth reflecting back the light of heaven,
Grows grand and beautiful, and calmly shines
On other worlds a bright and golden star.
And man himself is glorified, and raised
In dignity and living worth, when from
His spirit's deeps are mirrored back the love,
The truth, and rich beneficence of God.

Yonder, remote on the horizon's edge,
Bounding the widest range of roaming sight,
The dark-browed Mountains rise in majesty.
Wrapt in mysterious vests of misty blue,

They calmly look upon the world below,
With stern unbending gaze.

               Princes of earth
They stand, the emblems of enduring strength.
The storms that rock the deep and awe the world,
That rend and fling to earth the stalwart oak,
Or in their furious play to pieces dash
The giant ships, sweep over them in vain:
Sublime in strength, they scorn the wrecks of Time.

On every side, encircling woods present
A wreath of bright and gorgeous loveliness.
What nameless tints are beauteously inwrought
In the rich garland which the woodland wears!
The sombre brown and burning red combine
With the bright gold, the yet unfaded green,
And darker beauty of the queenly balsams;
Which proudly stand, fadeless amidst decay.
And fair as poet's dream, the maple grove,
Where every tree is drest with royal sheen,
Like brides with wreaths of orange blossoms crowned.
How many an eye, bright with the joy that floods
The throbbing heart, which now beholds these scenes
Of dying glory, never more shall see
The green leaves come again! How many an ear,
That has with calm delight drunk in
The pensive music of this autumn day,
Shall never hear the blessed songs of joy,
With which the birds shall welcome Spring's return!

Treading with rapt, unutterable joy,
The gorgeous carpet Autumn's gentle hand
Has spread beneath my feet, I wander on
In pensive day-dreams lost. I seem no more
The tenant of this lower world. I feel
As if some power invisible had raised
Me out of life and self, till from my throne
Of thought I muse upon myself, and all
The deep unfathomed mysteries of life,
With all the calm indifference of thought,
With which we muse on men beyond the flood.

Summer has gone. Her glory, like a dream,
Has waned and vanished from the mourning world.
Yet, here we roam through her deserted halls,
And, in the vestiges behind her left,
We see the tokens of her power, and catch
A glimpse of the magnificence, that marked
Her ardent and resplendent reign.

How like these scattered dying leaves,
So late the glory of the forest bowers,
Are all that wins the world's approving smile.
The chivalry of knightly souls, to whom
Honour and friendship were the crown of life,—
The toiling energy of hand and brain,—
The teachings of philosophy, and all
The art and skill of generations past,
Through which designs most godlike have been wrought,

Yea even the form and garb of truth itself,
And all that was the pride of other years,—
Have their brief season ; yet like autumn leaves,
Which die and disappear, but yet enrich
The soil for years to come, these transient forms,
Which disappear and seem to die, enrich
The world.   Although forgot, they share some part
In working out the world's high destiny.
They are the seeds of harvests yet to be,
Of finer fruitage and more perfect grain,
Destined to bless and beautify the world.

This place is holy ground.   A spoken word
Would jar the solemn harmony, that reigns
In these unruffled solitudes of peace.
'Tis more than joy to worship in this fane,
All built and fashioned by an unseen hand,
And silent listen to the holy symphonies,
That spirit voices whisper through the air,
When fading beauty speaks of nobler life,
Immortal, glorious, free from sorrow's blight ;
And Nature, hushed in reverential awe,
In mute devotion bows before her God.

JOHN MILTON.

AN ODE.

AIL patriot prince ! Bard of "the lofty rhyme!"
  Whose strains awaken deeper echoes, as they roll
Down the broad centuries of vanquished time :
  Thy bright example nerves the struggling soul,
  Who treads some thorny path with feet unshod;
  Thy lays ne'er fanned unholy passion's flame,—
The conscious presence of thy Maker, God,
  Was still the guardian of thy spotless fame.
    Who can tell his worth sublime,
    Living for all coming time ?
    Broad and deep prophetic vision
    Blend with calm and firm decision,
    Purpose high and faith divine
    All in his great soul combine,
    Girding, with mysterious power,
    For the stern, eventful hour,
    When, in Europe's wondering sight,
    Firm he battled for the right.

    When clouds were gathering round
    The isle to Freedom dear,
    And every threatening sound
    Betokened conflict near,
    Tyranny her minions armed,

And waved her banners gay—
Freedom and Truth, alarmed
At Error's fierce array,
To Heaven direct their prayer,
That, in the coming strife,
When Britain cast the die
For boon more dear than life,
To lead their hosts in fight
A champion might be given,
With fortitude and might,
And choicest gifts of heaven;—
Heaven heard their prayer, and, prompt to save,
To Truth and England MILTON gave.

Like some majestic oak, that rears its head
    High o'er its fellows of the forest wild,
And suns its boughs where cloudless light is shed,—
    King of the forest,—Nature's darling child—
So rises MILTON, of the regal mind,
    O'er all the tribe which sordid passions blind,
Till, from his throne of thought, with scorn he gazed
    On venial souls, who royal folly praised:
Bearing Truth's banner in the battle's van,
    His life maintained the dignity of man.

Like Leonidas the bold,
At Thermopylæ, of old,
King of patriot souls he stood,
Hero-hearted, great and good,
Dealing swift and heavy blows

To his country's faithless foes,
Till oppression's galling yoke
Was in shattered pieces broke.
Then the sacred pledge was given,
In the eyes of Earth and Heaven,
That through all the coming time
They should guard the gift sublime,
Never stoop to wear again
Kingly tyrant's yoke or chain.

As flies before the rising sun
Deep nightly gloom and shadows dun,
Till hills and vales emerge to sight,
Radiant in the morning light ;
So, in the glorious realms of thought,
Did Heaven unveil the truths he sought.
  As the solar rays
  Hide the lamps of night,
  In his radiant blaze
  Minor orbs were lost to sight.
  Through hopes and fears
  Of coming years,
Through mists of passion, prejudice, and pride,
  He saw afar
  Truth's guiding star,
And sternly scorned to seek another guide.
  Like a mirror in the night,—
  While the darkness shrouds below,—
  Turned to catch the starry light,
  And reflect its golden glow,

Sordid vices of his age
Do not stain his glowing page ;—
Not the darkness of his time
Is reflected in his rhyme,
But the blessed orbs above,
Founts of holy light and love,
Shed o'er his poetic dreams
Beauty's pure and peaceful beams.

But Folly seized again the helm of state,
And Freedom bowed beneath the stroke of Fate ;
Back to the throne the faithless exile came ;
Dishonoured Virtue wept o'er England's shame ;
Portentous shadows spread the future o'er,
And Freedom's soil was stained with patriot gore.
When darkness fell upon the beauteous world,
And Truth's fair banner was in sorrow furled,
When every form of beauty Earth displays
Was hid forever from his sightless gaze,
Though dim the hopeful visions of his youth,
Though proud oppression scorned his honored name,
Calmly reposing in the might of Truth,
He left to Time and Heaven his work and fame.
When Vice and Folly riot round the throne,
Desponding hearts deem Liberty o'erthrown,
He knew from seeds in nights of darkness sown
In future ages Freedom's oaks should rise,
And wave majestic under cloudless skies.
In the lone darkness of his double night,

Within his spirit burned a holy light,
He plumed his pinions for sublimer flight;—
Poor, old, and blind, by royal minions spurned,
With joy serene to nobler themes he turned,
High o'er the sordid throng, triumphant rose
With calm disdain, forgetful of his woes;
Though earthly beauty midnight gloom conceals,
Celestial grandeur kindly Heaven reveals.

In that pure height,
Immortal light
Wraps his great soul in joy and wonder,
The wild commotion
Of life's rough ocean,
Its sounds of gladness,
And moans of sadness,
Are heard afar, like distant thunder.

Then in his breast bright flamed the sacred fire,—
And starry thoughts upon his darkness shine,
He strung his harp to melody divine,
And from its chords seraphic music flung,
Heedless of praise or blame, he calmly sung
Such strains, as ne'er were heard from mortal lyre.

Angels of heaven above
Bent from their thrones of love—
Such grace to them is given—
And wondering, round the poet throng,
Whose life was lofty as his song,
Amazed to hear a child of time,
In his pure and deathless rhyme,
Rival the songs of heaven.

Hail immortal poet-king!
Thou has borne us on thy wing
Through the starry realms of thought,
Where the wars of heaven were fought,—
Far above the surge of care,
Thrilled with visions grand and rare,—
Hast unveiled the deeps of hell,
Held with weird and wondrous spell,
Singing of the power and pride,
Which the King of heaven defied—
Giant angels in their might
Closing in celestial fight,
Till, through chaos, down to hell,
Thrust in stygian gloom to dwell.
Then, by wily Satan led,
Over earth their gloom they spread,
Bringing on our hapless race
Loss of Eden, foul disgrace.

Sweeter strains our fears dispel,
As he sings of Christ, our King,
Who o'ercame the powers of hell,
Wrung from Death his fatal sting,
Rescued from our dark disgrace,
And, in pure and peerless love,
Ope'd the gates of heaven above
To our guilty, suffering race.
Like some pure and peaceful river,
Flowing on and on forever,
Thousands in the past have drank

At its cool and verdant bank,
In the future thousands more
Never shall exhaust its store,
Though they drain with grateful pride
Cups of gladness from its tide.
  Still his words of fire
  Ring in mortal ears,
  And his magic lyre
  Pours along the years
  Peals of melody and love,
  Grand as hymns of heaven above.
  Though he sleeps in dust,
  Yet each burning thought,
  Which inspired his trust,
  Into life is wrought,
  And appears anew
  In each heart sincere,
  That to God is true
  In its life-work here.

In lofty life and minstrelsy sublime,
He sits enthroned o'er all the bards of time.
In the great battle for the right he rose,—
Stern and invincible to freedom's foes,—
A lofty rock amid the surging main,
On which the wrathful billows beat in vain.

Songs of the World Without.

SHADOWS ON THE CURTAIN.

Awoke from the dreams of the night,
From restful and tranquil repose,
And looked where the sunbeams lay bright,
To see what the morn might disclose.
My window looked out on the east,
And opened to welcome the Sun,
As he rose, from the darkness released,
All girded, his journey to run.
I watched, as I lay,
The leaf-shadows play—
For the trees were still mantled in green—
As they silently danced,
Curvetted and pranced,
On the curtain, suspended between.

Then I said to my soul, "here's some thought
For thee to decipher and read:
Every form, that in nature is wrought,
Bears some lesson to those who give heed.
Between our weak eyes and the light
A thick-woven curtain is spread;

All the future it screens from our sight,
　And the home and the fate of the dead.
　　　The phantoms which still
　　　With perplexity chill,
Which doubting Despondency brings,
　　　Are cast, as they shine,
　　　By the sunbeams divine,
And are shadows of beautiful things."

Then I drew the broad curtain aside,
　And looked out on the beautiful world ;
The dew-drops were flashing, and wide
　Were the banners of beauty unfurl'd.
The leaves, that had silently flung
　Their shadows to darken my room,
Each answered with musical tongue
　To the zephyrs, that play'd with its bloom.
　　　And thus may it be,
　　　At life's ending with me ;
When Death rends the curtain away,
　　　May I rise to behold,
　　　In beauty unroll'd,
The morn of a shadowless Day.

SUMMER RAMBLES.

ITY clangors are far behind us,
    Dusty streets and noisome air ;
Ruthless Toil can no longer bind us—
    Liberty shatters the gyves of care.

Over the hills and valleys straying,
    Joy-flush'd and buoyant—Herbert and I—
Soothed by the summer-winds, softly playing,
    Are drinking gladness with ear and eye.

Green are the hills which the clouds float over—
    Mountains of pearl in a sapphire sea—
Zephyrs are laden with scent of clover,
    And rural melodies, blythe and free.

In maple and beech, in summer glory—
    Altars of praise, for jubilant song —
Bird to bird seems telling some story,
    Which thrills and gladdens the warbling throng.

Herds of cattle, in grassy meadows,
    Mottling the valleys, recline at ease,—
Ruminate dreamily under the shadows,
    Cast by the graceful, sheltering trees.

Orchards laden with apples and peaches—
   Fields are white with the waving grain—
Fading blossoms silently teach us
   Lessons which thought shall long retain.

Here and there, by the trees half-hidden,
   We catch a glimpse of some pleasant home ;
And the thought springs up to the lips unbidden,
   "O why should Canada's children roam ?"

Silver streams, over pebbles gliding,
   Ripple and flash in the evening ray ;
Emblems of candor which, nothing hiding,
   Opens its heart to the light of day.

Leaning here on the bridge to rest me,
   Watching the waters which glide below,
Joys of my childhood rise to bless me,
   Streams that seem'd beautiful long ago.

Throbbing with deep, unworded gladness
   And bounding life, is forest and field ;
Sights and sounds, full of balm for sadness,
   Rustic rambles lavishly yield.

Soul-soothed, I gaze on encircling beauty,
   Passive and dreamy, yet life shall win
A picture of joy, that shall lighten duty,
   And blend its songs with the city's din.

THE POLAR SEA.

SUPPOSED TO BE SPOKEN, BY MORTON OF DR. KANE'S EXPEDITION,
IN SIGHT OF THE OPEN POLAR SEA.

ID frost-built palaces of crystal rocks,
    I gaze with silent, wondering awe,
Upon this nameless sea, which Winter locks,
    In bonds that never thaw.

Whence comes the genial breath, that strangely frees
    The billows of this mystic main ;
While unrelenting Frost, o'er Southern seas,
    Maintains unbroken reign.

To mortal eye was ne'er unveiled before
    An earthly vision so sublime !
Stern Nature marks not, on this lifeless shore,
    The silent steps of Time.

No vessel built or steered by human art,
    Thy lonely tide has glided o'er ;
And, when my venturous feet shall hence depart,
    Thou mayst be seen no more.

Here Spring comes not, with buds of hope and song,
    Nor Summer fair, with blossoms crowned :
Save howling storms, that madly sweep along,
    Thou hearest no other sound.

These Winds, that wail o'er hills and plains of ice,
    Bear not upon their frozen wings
The scent of flowers, or sound of human voice,
    Or song of bird that sings.

Here iron Desolation sits enthroned,
    Where sullen Nature never smiled ;
But, like a heartless mother, has disowned
    And scorned her trusting child.

Yet, when the sun gleams through those icy walls,
    To each such gorgeous hues are given,
As might to wondering Poet's thoughts recall
    His brightest dream of heaven.

So full of mystery, and strangely wrought,
    The peerless vision spread to view,
That those who measure all things by their thought,
    May deem my tale untrue.

And Earth, has hearts like thee, O ! Sea, on whom
    Friendship and love have never shone ;
Who bear their burdens, through a life of gloom
    Companionless—alone.

Beneath these silent and eternal snows
    Brave Franklin and his comrades sleep :
Their hearts of fire have found serene repose—
    Their memory Fame shall keep.

No mortal eye beheld their anguish sore—
   No voice of kindness soothed or blest—
Of all whose friendship brightened life before,
   None knows their place of rest.

He only saw them sink in death's repose—
   Saw their deep sadness and despair—
Whose mercy tempers Sorrow's keenest woes,
   And hears Affliction's prayer.

And some, the Franklins in the world of mind,
   Searching, soul-hungry, fearless-hearted,
Have left their fellow-seekers far behind,
   From guiding way-marks parted;

And wandering far, through labyrinths of thought
   Profound, charmed with the flowers that bloom
In dim retreats, have sunk, at last, forgot,
   In solitude and gloom.

To these Columbus-hearted seekers pay,
   Whether they win the goal or fall,
Honour, regret, and gratitude, for they
   Are creditors of all.

Lone, melancholy Sea, thy pensive wail,
   So full of agony and strife,
Hath sung itself into my heart, and shall
   Forever haunt my life.

THE FALLS OF NIAGARA.

ERE yet I saw the wild magnificence,
   Which Nature here with peerless pomp unveils,
   A solemn sound—a stern and sullen roar—
   By which the earth was tremulously thrilled—
   Kindled a flush of deep, expectant joy,
   Quickening the pulses of my throbbing heart,
And tingling through my veins like fire. But now,
While standing on this rocky ledge, above
The vast abyss, which yawns beneath my feet,
In silent awe and rapture, face to face
With this bright vision of unearthly glory,
Which dwarfs all human pageantry and power,
This spot to me is Nature's holiest temple.
The sordid cares, the jarring strifes, and vain
Delights of earth are stilled. The hopes and joys
That gladden selfish hearts, seem nothing here.

The massy rocks that sternly tower aloft,
And stem the fury of the wrathful tide—
The impetuous leap of the resistless flood,
An avalanche of foaming, curbless rage—
The silent hills, God's tireless sentinels—
The wild and wondrous beauty of thy face,

Which foam and spray forever shroud, as if
Like thy Creator, God, thy glorious face
No mortal eye may see unveiled and live—
Are earthly signatures of power divine.
O! what are grandest works of mortal art,
Column, or arch, or vast cathedral dome,
To these majestic foot-prints of our God!

Unique in majesty and radiant might,
Earth has no emblems to portray thy splendor.
Not loftiest lay of earth-born bard could sing,
All that thy grandeur whispers to the heart
That feels thy power.   No words of mortal lips
Can fitly speak the wonder, reverence, joy—
The wild imaginings, thrilling and rare,
Which now, like spirits from some higher sphere,
For whom no earthly tongue has name or type,
Sweep through my soul in waves of surging thought.
My reason wrestles with a vague desire
To plunge into thy boiling foam, and blend
My being with thy wild sublimity.
As thy majestic beauty sublimates
My soul, I am ennobled while I gaze—
Warm tears of pensive joy gush from my eyes,
And grateful praise and worship silent swell,
Unbidden, from my thrilled and ravished breast;
Henceforth this beauteous vision shall be mine—
Daguerreotyped forever on my heart.

Stupendous power! thy thunder's solemn hymn
Whose tones rebuke the shallow unbeliefs
Of men, is still immutably the same.
Ages ere mortal eyes beheld thy glory,
Thy waves made music for the listening stars,
And angels paused in wonder as they passed,
To gaze upon thy weird and awful beauty,
Amazed to see such grandeur this side heaven.
Thousands, who once have here enraptured stood,
Forgotten, lie in death's lone pulseless sleep;
And when each beating heart on earth is stilled,
Thy tide shall roll, unchanged by flight of years,
Bright with the beauty of eternal youth.

Thy face, half-veiled in rainbows, mist, and foam,
Awakens thoughts of all the beautiful
And grand of earth, which stand through time and change
As witnesses of God's omnipotence.
The misty mountain, stern in regal pride,
The birth-place of the avalanche of death—
The grand old forests, through whose solemn aisles
The wintry winds their mournful requiems chant—
The mighty rivers rushing to the sea—
The thunder's peal—the lightning's awful glare—
The deep, wide sea, whose melancholy dirge,
From age to age yields melody divine—
The star-lit heavens, magnificent and vast,
Where suns and worlds in quenchless splendor blaze—
All terrible and beauteous things create
Are linked in holy brotherhood with thee,
6

And speak in tones above the din of earth
Of Him unseen, whose word created all.

God of Niagara !   Fountain of life !
At whose omnific word the universe
Arose ; whose love upholds all worlds, and guides
Each orb in its mysterious path through space ;
Around whose throne the Morning-stars of light
Bend low in wondering adoration, or
With lofty hymns of love and joy proclaim
Thy power and grace, boundless—immutable !
I, a poor erring worm of earth, a child
Of sin, am all unworthy to behold
This faint reflection of thy glorious power :
How, then, can I approach thy glorious throne,
Or dare to breathe in thine offended ear
The wants and woes of my polluted heart ?

Father of mercy ! hear my trembling prayer !
To me let love and light divine be given,
To guide my erring feet in paths of truth,
And purify my dark and sin-stained heart ;
That while I muse upon thy glorious works,
And mark the tokens of thy presence here,
I may behold Thyself, and find in Thee
My strength, my light, my everlasting Friend.

MORNING BELLS.

Stand 'mid the shadows of night,
    Watching the stars decay;
Softly they melt from my wondering sight,
    At the flush of the coming day.
Faintly at first the clouds give token,
    By the gleams of their kindling glow,
That the sceptre of Darkness and gloom is broken,
    And Light is enthroned below.

The morning bells are joyously ringing,
    Hailing the day with a gladsome chime;
And the birds as sweetly and merrily singing,
    As if this hour was the birth of time.
Dreamer awake from thy drowsy pillows—
    There are dewy diamonds on every spray:
The orient is gorgeous with golden billows,
    That are bathed in the new-born day.

The zephyr brings health on its balmy wing,
    The blue of the sky grows deeper,
And all the voices of Nature ring
    A call to the thoughtless sleeper.

Peal out, peal out, ye bells of the morning,
　Your chimes have a mystic meaning;
They are voices of hope, of joy, and warning,
　To the throngs that are slothfully dreaming.

Voices of joy, which loudly proclaim
　That the shadows of Night have been banished;
And the phantoms of fear, which came in her train,
　At the footsteps of Morning have vanished.
Joy to the mothers, who watch and weep
　By sufferers with agony torn;
And joy to the sailor far out on the deep,
　Who longs for the coming of morn.

Voices of duty, your music falls:
　The hours of repose are gone;
And we hear a voice in each stroke, that calls
　To work till the night comes on.
Ye call the soul from its baseless dreams
　To the toilful struggles of life,
That the morning's fresh and dewy beams
　May nerve for the coming strife.

There are fields to be ploughed, now rough and bare,
　Ere the seed of truth can be sown,
And weary hours of watching and care,
　Ere the golden sheaves are grown.
There is patient toil in the mines of thought,
　Ere the seeker's work is done;

And battles on gory fields to be fought,
  Ere the victor's crown can be won.

Voices of hope, for this opening day
  Will shed blessings on many a sphere;
And signals of care and deep dismay,
  For danger and death may be near.
It may be joy and the victor's crown,
  A sunset bathed in gladness;
Or it may be our sun shall at eve go down
  In clouds of despair and sadness.

There are signal bells in life's dewy morn,
  Ringing warnings loud and clear,
Whose echoes are swiftly and solemnly borne
  By Heaven to each youthful ear;
And to him who hears with thoughtful soul
  Those voices of truth and love
Shall life's evening bells bring a peaceful goal
  As the earnest of rest above.

THE ATLANTIC CABLE.

RING out the loud acclaim !
　　A grander victory claims each iron tongue,
Than ever warrior won on field of fame,
　　　　Or poet sung.

　　Birth of an age sublime,
To whose unsealed and Heaven-illumed eye,
New worlds of thought, the starry spheres of Time,
　　　　Unshrouded lie.

　　Waiting this latter day,
Like undiscovered mines, descried at last,
What giant forces hid in Nature lay
　　　　Through ages past !

　　What ancient days saw not,
By Heaven long sealed from mortal eye and ear,
Unpierced by poet's deep prophetic thought,
　　　　We see and hear.

　　The thrilling tale is told,
Which doth the world's dull listless ear command ;
The child at play—the miser o'er his gold—
　　　　All wondering stand.

A belt of thought has spanned
The deep. While storms above resistless roll,
Across a dim and undiscovered land,
    Soul speaks to soul.

Frail link, thy path is strange,
Silent and lone by mortal foot untrod;
In darkness hidden from light's deepest range,
    Known but to God:

O'er mountains sunk from sight,
Whose highest peaks are sunny sea-girt isles,
Through valleys lit with gleams of pearly light,
    Where beauty smiles:

Where sleep the dead unknown,
In caverns lone, deep-hid from Friendship's eye;
Where no green mound, nor monumental stone,
    Tells where they lie.

Tidings of victory won,—
Of kingdoms lost and proudest hopes laid low,
Along thy secret path shall swiftly run
    To thrill with joy or woe.

Thy mystic whisper shall
Kindle the light of gladness in the breast,
And cause the tear of agony to fall
    From hearts distrest.

We fain would know from thee,
What scenes of grandeur and of beauty lie
Hid, in the bosom of the "sounding sea,"
From mortal eye.

Our questionings are vain.
Mysterious herald, thou wilt not forego
Those treasured secrets of the mighty main,
We long to know.

With wondering joy we see
The grand achievement patient toil has wrought ;
The world beholds with awe the majesty
Of human thought.

May Art's great triumph prove
A golden bond, by our great Father given,
To bind two worlds in amity and love,
By time unriven ;—

A tie of brotherhood—
A vital ligament, through which shall flow
Thoughts, that promote the peace and good
Of all below.

HOMEWARD BOUND.

Long farewell to India's strand,—
  To the torrid eastern world,
Was waved by many a British hand,
  From a ship with flags unfurled;
For those who have toiled with tireless strife
  For fortune's withering bays,
Are returning to spend the Autumn of life
  In the scenes of their vernal days.

    *   *   *   *   *   *

'Tis the sunset hour, but the sun is hid
  'Neath a veil of sombre-hued gray,
Not a sun-lit rock, or bird-song to bid
  Farewell to a gloom-laden day.
The sorrowful spirit of sky and sea
  On the world has drearily fell—
No fisherman's voice has its wonted glee,
  As he lists to the ocean swell.

The storm is less fierce, but the mountain waves
  Still roll o'er the foaming tide,
And break in snow on the rocky caves,
  That a thousand storms have defied;—

As if wroth with the winds that disturb their rest,
  They shriek out their desolate moan,
Till the Deep seems a fellow spirit, opprest
  With unspeakable woes of its own.

There is grandeur and terror beyond compare,
  When the Storm-fiends wrathfully rave,
And the mammoth ship, like a leaf of air,
  Is tossed by the giant wave;
Yet, even in moods of wildest ire,
  Is no sterner majesty shown,
Than after the hurricane blasts retire,
  When each billow rolls sullen and lone.

Then the fishermen mend their nets in hope
  That the tempest is passing away,—
Till Night comes down with an eagle swoop,
  And seizes the world as her prey:
Then at home they talk of the perilous deep,—
  Of the storms of the toil-haunted years,
Till the memory of those, whom the billows keep,
  Bedews rugged faces with tears.

Hark! a thrilling sound, through the twilight gloom,
  To the fisherman's ear is given—
'Tis a signal gun, like a knell of doom
  From a vessel shore-ward driven—
She is seen through the gloom, like a sea-gull afar,
  Nor compass nor helm doth guide—

Of power bereft, like a broken spar
   She is swept by the seething tide.

Mirk clouds spread their sable wings below,
   And the vessel is hidden from sight ;
Still the signal guns toll their notes of woe
   In the ear of the pitiless Night.
And yet, though her fate moves each manly heart,
   As she comes toward the death-dealing reef,
In that rayless storm no courage nor art
   Can rescue or bring relief.

Alas! brave ship, though gallant thy crew,
   Though nigh to the haven they sought,
Though freighted with hopeful hearts and true,
   Thy peril appalleth thought ;—
For the night is dark, and the waves run high,
   The coast is rocky and bare,
And the shore that gladdened each weary eye,
   Is shrouded by Night and Despair.

The Morning dawns with a smile of peace
   Over ocean, and earth, and sky.
The terrible wails of the breakers cease,
   Softly changed to a mournful sigh.
The mountains gleam in the golden ray,
   And the fields look glad as of yore ;
The song of the fisher is heard on the bay,
   And the song of the birds on the shore.

But the storm-swept ship has bowed to fate—
　　She will plough the blue deep no more !
The relenting waves bear her precious freight
　　Wrapt in sea-weed shrouds to the shore.
The lifeless forms that she bore, are left
　　On the sands of the treacherous main,
And the hearts that the ire of the storm has bereft,
　　Shall keep watch for their coming in vain.

There the mother sleeps by her infant pearls,
　　And the youth in his manly pride—
The hoary head—and the flaxen curls—
　　And the hopeful and beautiful bride—
O ! why was He whom the winds obey,
　　Unmoved by their anguish and strife ?
We can only tell when eternal Day
　　Shall illumine the problems of life.

AUTUMNAL MEMORIES.

SUMMER has vanished, with her winsome glory
    Of emerald woods, and fields besprent with flowers.
These scattered leaves proclaim the mournful story
    Of naked trees, and desolated bowers.

Erewhile, autumnal beauty, soft and mellow,
    Fell on the landscape like a vision bright;
When ruby tints, with green and gorgeous yellow,
    Were gaily wove in coronals of light.

Through golden haze the noiseless hours were winging—
    Banners of flame from every hill were flung—
From morn till night, echoes of joy and singing
    Through all the forest arches sweetly rung.

The crimson maple blushed a forest queen,
    Or rose transfigured to a golden cone:
Like brilliant tassels, through the leafy green,
    The scarlet berries of the rowans shone.

Then bounteous Autumn came with treasures laden—
    Red apples, purple grapes, and yellow grain—
All richest gifts—till, like a fruitful Aden,
    Earth seemed restored to primal bliss again.

Those dreamy, melancholy days are over,—
　　The peaceful sunset of the waning year.
We part from brooding, golden-robed October,
　　With kind farewells, and with regrets sincere.

All day the farmer ploughs the naked fallow—
　　With patient skill furrows the loamy soil,
And fills the hours with pleasant thoughts, which hallow
　　And cheer his weary, Heaven-appointed toil.

Gray, murky skies o'erhang the dull November.
　　There's sorrow in the murmurs of the rain,
And wailing winds, which bid the heart remember
　　The dreary homes of poverty and pain.

In sunny intervals gay shouts are breaking—
　　The farewell plaudits which the year receives—
From noisy urchins, in the woodlands seeking
　　For fallen beech-nuts, 'neath the wither'd leaves.

Thus softly gliding, as the steps of angels,
　　The seasons come and go at God's command;
Bringing to thankful hearts their glad evangels,
　　And rich love-tokens from our Father's hand.

All seasons magnify His grace and glory.
　　Spring's dewy blossoms, Summer's living green,
Autumn's ripe fruits, and Winter wild and hoary—
　　In each supernal love and power are seen.

THE ROBIN'S STORY.

SINCE early morn a robin has sung,
  In the boughs of yon maple tree;
My heart is touched by her melody, flung
  Like a pearl on a heedless sea.
    She seems to complain,
    Sitting lonely apart;
    There's a tone in her strain,
    That must come from the heart;
And the heart must be full, that so long
Could have prompted and fed such a song.

I fain would know what the robin says,—
  The tale that she seems to tell.
No mate is near; and it is not praise;
  For each note has a mournful swell.
    Thus my fancy wrought,—
    To the robin's lay
    Wedding words and thought,
    Till she seemed to say :—
" My heart is crushed with a burden of grief,
Let me sing my woes, it may yield relief.

In Spring, how happy and gay was my life,—
  My mate was both loving and true,

I built my nest, like a thrifty wife,
  In a beech, where the sun peept through :
      With soft grasses press'd,
      And the finest clay,—
      In a sweeter nest
      Never wood-bird lay ;
And my sweet-heart true was so proud to see,
That a nest so fair had been built by me.

Soon four sweet eggs, as blue as the sky,
  To my heart gave a new delight;
And my husband sweetly sang close by,
  Till the sun went to sleep at night.
      In the beautiful May,
      At an early hour,
      One sorrowful day,
      We had left our bower ;
Together we flew, in quest of food,
Through the leafy haunts of the cool green wood.

And there my consort was shot by my side,
  And I, who had only he,
Was left, a desolate, widow'd bride,
  And forced, in dismay, to flee.
      I flew to my nest,
      To hide and to weep ;
      Bereaved and distrest,
      Scarce wing could I keep ;
The griefs of that hour, to memory seem,
Like thoughts of a dark, bewildering dream.

Alas! when I came to my own beech tree,
  The home once so fair and sweet,
None can picture the woe that harrowed me,
  The fate I was doomed to meet.
        My beautiful nest,
        By some wicked wight,
        Was torn from its rest,
        And—O woeful sight!
A wretched ruin was scattered around,—
My eggs lay broken and crush'd on the ground.

The friend of my heart, ineffably dear,
  Is ruthlessly torn from my side:
His sweet vesper song shall never more cheer,
  Or gladden his desolate bride.
        A poor, homeless thing,
        Whose life's-star is set,
        I can now only sing,
        In despair and regret.
May the wretches who blighted my lot,
Never feel the despair they have wrought."

OCEAN MUSINGS.

NTAMED, unresting deep, entranced I stand
Upon thy rocky shore, and watch thy waves
Laving with ceaseless surge the pebbly strand,
As they have surged for ages past. As slaves
For freedom long, I in my forest land,
Far from the music of these ocean caves,
Have fondly yearned, since childhood's early hour,
To gaze on thy immensity and peerless power.

With thrilled and heaving breast I greet thee now—
Beauty and grandeur charm my wondering eye—
Thy cooling breath is on my throbbing brow,—
The mournful music which thy waves supply
Fills my whole being, till o'erwhelmed I bow
To Him, whose greatness ocean, earth, and sky
To mortal hearts with varied voice proclaim;
In wisdom, love, and power, through every age the same.

Thou art a glorious harp, whose strings
Are touched by an unseen Almighty hand;
Whose plaintive voice forever grandly sings
Of Him, whose word created sea and land,
To the full chorus of those billows grand,
Earth's noblest melodies are feeble things;—

A solemn dirge to silence Folly's mirth,
A wail that utters all the wretchedness of Earth.

The hand of man in its resistless sway
Changes the world.   Before his enterprize
And patient toil the forests pass away,
And cities in the wilderness arise.
But fleets, that cross thy breast with pennons gay,
Leave thee as trackless as the starry skies :
No human power is suffered to maintain
A monument of majesty in thy domain.

Here warlike fleets have met in fierce array,
And human blood has crimsoned o'er thy tide ;
Treasures secluded from the light of day,
And thrilling secrets in thy bosom hide.
What wails of agony and wild dismay
Thy ear alone has heard, when hope had died !
What deeds of darkness, villiany, and crime,
Thy billows shroud forever from the eye of Time !

When the broad firmament is cloudless seen,
Responsive calm broods o'er thy burnished breast;
When golden stars begem the midnight scene •
Their glow is mirrored on thy azure vest;
When clouds and storms disturb the blue serene
Of heaven, thy sympathy is soon confest,
Thy brow grows dark, thy billows wildly leap,
And o'er thy desert plains unpitying tempests sweep.

As on this lonely shore with joy I roam,
Lulled by the music of this ceaseless moan,
Watching the billows break in snowy foam
Against the rocks—alone, yet not alone,
With ocean in her pensive moods at home,
On wings of musing fancy I have flown
Into the world of dreamy thought.   The war
Of selfish strife I hear like echoes faint and far.

Wide restless Sea, thy majesty divine
Has stirred the deeps of feeling in my breast,
And kindled thoughts, which memory shall enshrine,
Like words of love by lips of truth confest.
Only the soul has grandeur vast as thine,—
Has storms as wild, and moods of tranquil rest,
Battles as fierce as naval records keep,
And pearls as rich as in thy secret caverns sleep.

And when, in meditative, peaceful mood,
I wander over green Canadian hills,
Or, in the deep recesses of our grand old wood,
Hear the low song of unfrequented rills,
The vision of this restless heaving flood,
Whose glory now with pensive gladness fills,
Shall still through winter's snow, or summer's glare,
Live in my thoughts, and yield an anodyne for care.

THE HUNTER TO HIS BRIDE.

COME away with me
   To the forest free,
From the world with its jarring strife,
   Where Envy's sneers
   And Sorrow's tears
Embitter and darken life. ♥
      In the grand old woods
      No Envy intrudes,
   And Beauty is chosen queen—
      There the wood-birds sing,
      And the crystal spring
   Sparkles with silvery sheen.

      I know where the shade
      By the evergreens made,
   Shall shelter thy throbbing head—
      Where the wild-berries grow,
      And the broad rivers flow,
   And the cool, mossy seats are spread;
      Where the honey-bees bring
      The sweets of the Spring,
   And treasure the wealth they gain;
      And the cooling breeze,
      As it plays through the trees,

Soothes the heart with its tender strain.
There the partridges drum
When the Spring has come,
And the wild-flowers bloom in pride,
And the bright lakes are seen
Among hills of green,
With a glassy and waveless tide.

Come away with me
To the forest free,
From the selfish and soul-less throng,
Who struggle for gold
Till the heart is cold,
And seared by falsehood and wrong.
Though no costly fare
Nor adornings rare,
No treasures of gold are mine,
I will give thee a heart
Free from guileful art,
That is fondly and faithfully thine.

In the genial Spring,
When the zephyrs bring
New life to the sleeping world,
When the silver streams
Awake from their dreams,
And the leafy flags are unfurled,
In the green-shaded bowers
We will wreath the young flowers,

And sit where the rivulets glide,
 While the birds sing above
 Sweet sonnets of love,
To give joy to my fair, forest bride.

 When the autumn hours
 Have tinted the bowers,
With golden and crimson dyes,
 And rich Nature pours
 Her bountiful stores
To gladden our grateful eyes,—
 When the fading leaves
 And the tranquil eves
Softly whisper of life's decline,
 Our hymns of praise,
 With the wild-bird's lays,
Shall rise to the Father divine.

 And when Winter proud
 Spreads his ermine shroud
Over Nature's unbroken repose.
 On our snow-shoes light
 We will range with delight
O'er the deep and the stainless snows.
 I will build our cot
 In some sheltered spot,
From Care and Ambition free ;
 And the wolf-skin spread
 For thy dreaming head,
On soft boughs of the hemlock tree.

Then our waking dreams,
Like meandering streams,
Shall glide through the vales of thought;
And our tranquil minds
May thought-pearls find,
Which monarchs have vainly sought ;
For the toiling brain
Often labours in vain,
And is clouded at last by despair—
Then come with me
To the forest free,
And escape from the haunts of Care.

ODE TO IMAGINATION.

I.

ETHEREAL spirit of celestial birth,
　　Parent of golden dreams and thoughts sublime,
　　Whose lustre brightens the dark stream of Time;
Thou dost on wings of rapture visit Earth,
　　And from her dark, unsightly fibres weave
　　Vestments of glory for terrestrial things,
Which, like the tints that gild the clouds of Eve,
　Are the bright gleams celestial radiance flings
Around the sombre dwelling of the soul.
Inspire my feeble song, my thoughts control,
　　That I in worthy notes may raise
　　My tuneful pæan to thy praise;
　　And yield a tribute glad and free
　　For all the joyance thou hast given to me;
For thou, alone, canst mortal minstrel dower
With skill, to sing the mystery of thy power.

II.

To sing thy power, would claim a seraph's tongue,
　And thought and melody of loftier tone
Than ever yet from earthly harp has rung,—
　Grand as the ocean's tempest-wafted moan,—
To voice in harmony thy wondrous art.

Thou dost with light the filmy eye illume,—
Dost wing the dull and mist-enveloped heart,
  To rise and pierce the thick, o'erhanging gloom;
And look with rapture on the stars that glow
  Serenely bright, while earth is dark below.
By thee, imprisoned thoughts, which gracious Heaven
  To this material universe has given,
    Break forth in melody divine :
    And flowers that fade, and stars that shine
    Sing thrilling hymns, which mortal ear
    Untouched by thee, could never hear;
Till form and beauty, by thy fingers wrought,
Fill up the dark, chaotic voids of thoughts.

III.

As, at the blush of Morning, swiftly rise
  From out the darkling shadows of the night,
Forest, and lake, and hill, in golden light
  Reflecting back the glories of the skies,
Imagination, child of Heaven, thy hand
  Unveils the beauty, harmony, and skill,
  Which the wide circle of creation fill.
Though hid from common gaze, at thy command
What mountains decked with crowns of sacred flame—
What boundless oceans, vast as thought can claim—
What fertile vales, and waving forests green—
Enchain the spirit with entrancing sheen.
With crudest ore, from mines of darkness brought,
  And rugged stones, quarried from common fate,
Building the stately palaces of thought,—

Fair as a vision of the blessed state,—
The pride and wonder of all future time,—
The deathless monuments of minds sublime.

IV:

Unto the ear thy magic touch unseals,
    Nature is eloquent with wordless thought;
    Her every voice with deepest wisdom fraught.
The Ocean's billows moan the woe she feels:
The Forest calls us to her calm retreat;
    The River sings its melody of joy,
And humbly bathes the toil-worn pilgrim's feet.
    Morning invites anew to life's employ;
And Sunset's splendor, with celestial art,
Pours soothing music on the weary heart.
The tranquil Autumn speaks of life's decline,—
Prophetic Spring, of loveliness divine;
        And Winter's stern, unpitying strife,
        Of the dark battle-field of life.
        Childhood, with stars of joy above,
        And Youth, with stars of life and love—
        All forms the wondering eye surveys,
        Which heaven above or earth displays—
        All sounds that greet the quickened ear,
        Vibrate with sympathy sincere,
When thou hast given communion, fresh as youth,
With every type of beauty, joy and truth.

V.

If o'er this lower world thy glance is thrown,
    The things inanimate with life are gifted.

From grandeur's form the shrouding veil is lifted;
And, charmed, we drink each rapture-breathing tone
Of forms, before silent and dark as night,
 Now preachers, eloquent, in Nature's fanes.
The rock-ribbed mountain, in thy wondrous light,
 A patriarchal monarch sternly reigns,
Frowning secure, when, from its misty peaks,
Thunder to thunder, answering, hoarsely speaks.
Unsleeping sentinels, they proudly stand,
Like giant spirits, watching o'er the land;
   While ever whispering, sweetly low,
   As distant music's softened flow,
   Lessons of steadfast trust to all,
   In Him who hears the lowliest call,
Who fixed their vast foundations firm and deep,
Whose searching eye is never dimm'd with sleep.

VI.

When over vanished years thy wand is waved,
 They yield their treasures to thy mystic light.
 The kingly tyrant, in his selfish might,
And conquering armies, by thy spell ungraved,
Come forth and live another fruitless life.
 As in a dream, gray Time gives back his youth,
And hero-hearts renew the noble strife,
 That gave the world rich legacies of truth.
In Fancy's barque I swiftly glide along,
 Down the broad stream of ages as it ran,
Lulled by the music of a voiceless song,
 I mark the deeds and destiny of man.

I hear the voices of the years,
Glad with joy, or choked with tears,
Yielding to the coming time
All they know of truth sublime,
Till I awake to bless with grateful soul,
The Power propitious, which unveils the whole.

VII.

O'er space, as time, thy power occult prevails,
  And far-off climes their varied scenes unfold.
  The cloud-veiled future, by thy touch unroll'd,
Presents its grandeur, till the spirit quails
At ghostly pictures of the hidden world,—
  Or else in dreary doubt and darkness steep ;
  For thou canst lift the soul with eagle sweep
To gaze where beauty's banners are unfurled,
And heaven's unseen delights unveiled, impart
New life to faith, and joy-gleams to the heart.
    In thine airy chariot borne,
    Poet-souls serenely float
    Through the golden gates of Morn,
    Over realms of thought remote.
    All that Truth and Reason tell
    Rise to life at Fancy's spell,
    As we watch with raptured awe
    Wondrous visions which they saw.

VIII.

Homer chants how battles rise,
From the glance of beauty's eyes ;
Milton, on his starry wings

Bears us heavenward, while he sings
How seraphic legions fell.
Eden's sinless beauties rise
'Neath the light of halcyon skies,
On his dark and sightless age ;
And the eloquence of hell
Rivals heaven's upon his page.
Shakspeare guides, with calm control,
Through the empire of the soul.
Or with gloomy Dante tread
Through the dwellings of the dead,
Till in Paradise we rest,
Safe with Beatrice the blest.

IX.

Thou wine elysian of the sluggish brain,
    Thou gleam of heaven's immortal fire,
Let sordid lips pronounce thy visions vain,
    Give me the sacred rapture they inspire.
For who could plod the leaden rounds of life,
    Without the sunshine of thy genial light?
Or hear the moan of ever surging strife,
    Without thy visions, beautiful and bright?
No songs of Hope could cheer life's sunless shore,
    Nor joys of Memory faded blooms restore;
Without thy joy-dreams life would be a tomb,
    A leafless forest and a songless stream,
A flowerless plain, o'erhung with clouds of gloom,
    Unblest with emerald bower or golden beam.

ON THE RIVER.

THE sun has gone down in liquid gold,
    On the Ottawa's gleaming breast;
And the silent Night has softly rolled
    The clouds from her starry vest.
        Not a sound is heard—
        Every warbling bird
Has silenced its tuneful lay,
        As with calm delight,
        In the morn's weird light,
I noiselessly float away.

As down the river I dreamily glide—
    The sparkling and moonlit river—
Not a ripple disturbs the glassy tide,
    Not a leaf is heard to quiver:
        The lamps of night
        Shed their trembling light,
With a tranquil and silvery glory,
        Over river and dell,
        Where the Zephyrs tell
To the Night their plaintive story.

I gently time my gleaming oar
    To music of joy-laden strains,

Which the silent woods, and listening shore
  Re-echo in soft refrains.
     Let saintly thought,
     From this tranquil spot,
Float up through the slumbering air;
     For who would profane
     With fancies vain,
A scene so ineffably fair?

Now dark-browed, sorrowful Care retires,
  And leaves the bright moments unclouded—
For why should I shade them with vain desires,
  For hopes which the darkness has shrouded?
     Like phantoms grim,
     From the river's brim,
The trees stretch their shadows before me,—
     But no shadow jars,
     For the blessed stars
Are tenderly beaming o'er me.

On the dark and rapid river of life,
  Fall shadows of grief and sin,
But we reck not the gloom of the outer strife,
  If no shadows obscure within;
     Though darkness may lower,
     It is reft of power
Over hearts that are tempered with love;—
     There is fadeless light
     For life's darkest night,
With the bountiful Father above.

Songs of the World Within.

THROUGH THE SHADOWS.

THE sun has sunk below
    The mountains of the west,
The twilight shadows softly fall
    On blue Ontario's breast,
Till lake and hills are hid from from sight,
Beneath the dusky wings of Night.

While shadows fall without,
    And nature sinks to rest,
Shadows of anxious fear and doubt
    Gather within my breast;
As outward forms elude my eyes,
An inner world my soul descries.

Beneath the kindly shade
    Of calm and soothing Night,
I ponder o'er the vast unknown,
    And vainly seek for light;—
Questions come trooping through my soul,
I cannot answer nor control.

8

Why am I like a leaf
  By Autumn zephyrs driven,
Sometimes toward darkness and despair,
  And sometimes nearer heaven?
And why, as years of mercy flee,
Am I so far my God from Thee?

When adverse fate befalls,
  And earthly stars grow faint,—
When Sorrow's billows o'er me roll,
  I pour my sad complaint;
And purpose with sincere intent,
My life shall all for heaven be spent.

At times my faith grows strong,
  I scorn each threatening foe;
My life is all a pleasant song,
  To music's sweetest flow
Set by the power of faith and love,
Which lifts all earthly cares above.

Then on my raptured ear
  Celestial music falls,
All that my grateful eyes behold,
  Homeward and heavenward calls;
So vast my Father's love appears,
I wonder at my baseless fears.

But sombre hours come on,
  With stealthy mystic tread,

And quench the beacon lights of home,
  And murky shadows spread,
Till Faith has hushed her joyous hymn,
And all the stars of Hope grow dim.

The solid earth below
  Trembles beneath my feet,
And stern unpitying skies
  My upward glances meet:
The truths, I thought would aye abide,
Totter and reel on every side.

In doubt and gloom I grope
  My rough and toilsome way,
Hoping, with anxious trembling hope,
  That though I sadly stray,
My Father's eye, from heaven above,
Looks on my helplessness in love.

The bowers of other days,
  Have withered from my sight,
The streams from which I drank are dry,
  And, in my hopeless plight,
The vanished hours of gladness seem
Only a dim and baseless dream.

But why should I regret
  A loss that may be gain;
If many a meteor light has set,
  The sun and stars remain.

Though earthly waymarks fade from sight,
The heavens are gemmed with living light.

In darkness idle fears
　Are still of weakness born;
But darkness, doubts, and tears
　Shall vanish with the morn;
Though fainting, fearing, still I may
On God my trembling spirit stay.

Deep in my heart I feel
　That He is full of grace,
And, more than mortal words can tell,
　He loves our fallen race.
He will not leave in lone despair,
A soul that hangs upon his care?

When clouds obscure from sight
　The golden stars above,
And pain and sorrow sadly blight
　The flowers of earthly love,
Enough to know, that He will guide
To realms where fadeless joys abide.

Content, I weep no more,
　My times are in his hand;
'Mid angry billows, far from shore,
　He'll guide me safe to land;
Though doubts perplex and shadows lower,
I'll trust His wisdom, love, and power.

GOD'S HEROES.

" If any man serve me, him will my Father honor.—John xii. 26."

OT on the gory fields of fame
   Their noble deeds were done;
Not in the sound of Earth's acclaim
   Their fadeless crowns were won.
Not from the palaces of Kings,
   Nor Fortune's sunny clime,
Came the great souls, whose life-work flings
   Lustre o'er Earth and Time.

For Truth with tireless zeal they sought,—
   In joyless paths they trod—
Heedless of praise or blame they wrought,
   And left the rest to God.
The lowliest sphere was not disdained—
   Where love could soothe or save
They went, by fearless faith sustained,
   Nor knew their deeds were brave.

The foes with which they waged their strife
   Were Passion, Self, and Sin—
The victories, that laureled life,
   Were fought and won within.

Not names in gold emblazoned here,
  And great and good confest,
In Heaven's immortal scroll appear
  As noblest and as best.

No sculptured stone in stately temple
  Proclaims their rugged lot,—
Like Him who was their great example,
  This vain world knew them not.
But, though their names no poet wove
  In deathless song or story,
Their record is inscribed above—
  Their wreaths are crowns of glory.

The deeds which selfish hearts approve,
  And Fame's loud trumpet sings,
Secure no praise, where truth and love
  Are counted noblest things ;
And work which godless Folly deems
  Worthless, obscure, and lowly,
To Heaven's unerring vision seems
  Most god-like, grand, and holy.

Then murmur not, if toils obscure,
  And thorny paths be thine ;
To God be true—they shall secure
  The joy of life divine,
Who in the darkest, sternest sphere
  For him their powers employ ;—

The toils contemned and slighted here
  Shall yield the purest joy.

When endless Day dispels the strife
  Which blinds and darkens now,
Perchance the brightest crown of life
  Shall deck some lowly brow.
Then learn, despite thy boding fears,
  From seed with sorrow sown,
In lone obscurity and tears,
  The richest sheaves are grown.

———

CHRISTIAN WORK.

"Inasmuch as ye have done it unto one of the least of these my
brethren, ye have done it unto me.—Matt. xxv. 40.

GO while the light is beaming,
    Ere the evening shadows fall;
  Rest not in idle dreaming,
    While want and suff'ring call.
  Gloom and gladness here are blended—
    Earth has many a dreary lot—
  Rise and work till life be ended—
    Hearts are bleeding—linger not.

Go where poverty and sickness
  Shroud the poor in lonely grief;

Wake the sleeping pulse of gladness,
  Bring the fainting hearts relief.
Tho' their fate be dark and lonely,
  God still watches o'er the poor;
And, to those who kindly aid them,
  Heaven's sweet promises are sure.

Let the gifts thy God hath lent thee,
  Freely from His gracious hand,
Still be used as best thou knowest
  Will fulfil His wise command.
Every act of faithful duty—
  Every gift of kindly love,
Blossoms in immortal beauty
  In the world of life above.

Go where dreary darkness lingers
  O'er the life with dire control,
Loose with love's untiring fingers
  Every fetter of the soul.
Pour the light of truth around thee,
  Tell the story of the Cross—
Lest thy slothful, selfish folly
  Cause a soul's eternal loss.

Shall a godlike soul immortal,
  Once redeemed by blood divine,
Fail to pass the pearly portal,
  Lost through faithlessness of thine ?

Shall the friends who walked beside thee,
  Thro' thy pilgrimage below,
Say thou never once besought them
  To escape the coming woe ?

Go where sadly sink the dying,
  ˙In the shades of lone despair :
Hush the voice of hopeless sighing,
  Speak of hope and mercy there ;
Till the soul, as truth enlightens,
  Faith and love with joy inspire ;
And the hope of glory brightens,
  As the lights of earth expire.

So shalt thou, when life is waning,
  Gratefully the past review ;
And from heaven new strength obtaining,
  Still with joy thy way pursue.
And when Death thy life invading,
  Calls to quit thy work of love,
Home to purest joys unfading
  Christ shall welcome thee above.

FROM DARKNESS TO LIGHT.

"To turn them from darkness to light, and from the power of Satan
unto God."—Acts xxvi. 18.

PART I.—Twilight.

IKE one who follows, in the night,
The gleam of some misleading light,
Until it vanisheth from sight,

And leaves him, hopeless and forlorn.
By doubt and danger sorely torn,
Waiting and longing for the morn;

So have the lights, I followed, died;—
Ambition, selfish love, and pride
Can only into darkness guide.

I sought for joy in shallow streams,
That flashed 'neath hope's delusive beams,
But left me only fruitless dreams.

The flowers I thought would bloom for aye,
And ever fresh and fragrant stay,
Withered to dust with swift decay.

I sought for happiness in gay
And festive scenes, where night and day
On wings of pleasure fled away;

But, when the hours of mirth had gone,
A shadow fell my soul upon,
And, while it mocked me, goaded on.

Why do our cherished joys still turn
To dust and vapor, while they burn,
And leave the heart a joyless urn,

Haunted by gloomy, ghostly fears,
To keep the ashes of the years,
Watered by vain, regretful tears?

In sacred rites, I sought to find
If aught in holy forms enshrined
Could heal a dark, diseasèd mind.

I sought for happiness in lore
Of olden times, from minds which bore
Rich fruits of thought, an ample store

To enrich the world through coming time:
But neither poet's pensive rhyme,
Nor lore discursive and sublime,

Can lay the restless, shadowy fears,
That rise from out the murdered years,
Or dry the heart's unwitnessed tears.

The Past springs up, a threatening ghost—
My present thoughts, a guilty host—
And yet, the Future chills me most.

Though gloomy seems the path I've trod,
And rough the way where now I plod,
I, in the future, meet with God.

'Tis He whose care hath screened my head,
Who o'er my life his love hath spread,
And round my path His glory shed.

And yet, 'tis He whose grace I spurned;
From whom my reckless spirit turned,
When selfish pride and passion burned.

These grand, mysterious powers, within,
Must have some nobler work than sin;
Some higher victory to win,

Than to be Passion's menial slave,
Swept, by each changeful wind and wave,
On to a dark, oblivious grave.

Since Love is given, there must be, sure,
Some object beautiful and pure,
Which shall long as the soul endure;

To which the heart may safely cling,
From which the highest bliss shall spring,
Which shall o'er life a glory fling.

Since Faith is ours, exist there must
Some Being worthy of our trust,
That ne'er shall moulder into dust.

If Hope lies deep in every breast,
There must be gladness, joy, and rest,
Worthy the Soul's immortal quest.

I know that joy shall not be mine,
Till God within my spirit shine,
And heal my wounds with peace divine.

And yet, I cling to idle dreams,
I yield to Folly's baseless schemes,
And steer by Passion's meteor gleams.

I hush my anxious, secret fears,
Repress my sad and welling tears,
Till outward calm and peace appears.

Shrouding my inner gloom from sight,
I call my murky darkness light,
And wish my wrong could be the right.

At times, my soul her folly owns,
And secretly her want bemoans,
Yet shuts her ears to mercy's tones;

And seeks in doubt and disbelief,
To gain deliverance and relief
From her mysterious inner grief.

The arguments with which I seek
To hush the warning tones, which speak
Within my soul, are false and weak.

They are but passion's voice, and cower
Before the dawning, sun-lit hour,
When conscience speaks again with power.

PART II.—Midnight.

The way-marks all are hid from sight;
It is the depth of moonless night;
Ah! who shall guide my steps aright?

The memories of the wasted past
Gather around me, thick and fast,
And howl like shrieks of wintry blast.

The phantoms, which I followed long,
Which charmed with many a syren song,
Have led me far, in paths of wrong.

My sky is wrapt in starless gloom,—
I hear God's angry thunders boom,—
Before me gapes the loathesome tomb.

O Lord of Hosts! thou knowest my sin,
How vile and faithless I have been,
How deeply, darkly stained within.

Ten thousand times I heard thy voice,
Calling from folly's fatal choice,
Bidding me in Thyself rejoice.

I dare not lift my eyes to heaven—
I cannot hope to be forgiven—
I must be from thy glory driven.

Alas! I fear my sins will yet
Fill life eternal with regret,
When every star of hope has set.

There may be grace and mercy shed
On those by guileful error led,
Thoughtless how far from right they sped;

But I have sinned 'gainst love and light.
I heard the inner voice of right;
And chose the wrong, with keen delight.

My heart is burdened with despair—
My guilt is more than I can bear—
I look towards heaven—but God is there.

If He is holy, stern, and just,
How can the slave of sin and lust
Venture, in Him to hope or trust?

At times, in agony I plead,
That He would pity my soul's need,
And in the paths of mercy lead;

But, something whispers, " all is vain—
Too late! too late!" and then, with pain,
My hope is turned to doubt again.

My sins before me ever lie,—
Companions that can never die,—
I cannot from their presence fly.

When in the hallowed house of prayer,
All that the preacher's lips declare,
But feeds and strengthens my despair.

His words a voice of peace may be
To others, longing to be free,
But they, alas! are not for me.

Like shipwrecked sailor, in the night,
Catching some distant vessel's light,
Which swiftly vanishes from sight;

Tossed on a dark and stormy sea,
Betimes, some glimmering light I see,
Then deeper darkness covers me.

My heart seems harder than before:
The surging waves, which round me roar,
But bear me farther from the shore.

Drifting upon the bleak, wide sea
Of doubt, despair, and misery,
Yet from myself, I cannot flee.

So often have I hoped and tried,
And fairest flowers no fruit supplied,—
So often baffled, hope has died,

To my despairing heart, it seems
My hopes of peace are idle dreams,
Deceitful and misleading gleams.

And must I sink beneath my guilt?
Lord, thou canst save me if thou wilt—
For me a Saviour's blood was spilt.

In anguish sore thy grace I crave,—
A guilty rebel, Satan's slave,—
Thou only, Christ, canst hear and save.

PART III.—Dawn.

Still weary, watching for the morn,
In ebon darkness, faint and lorn—
When will the blessed day be born?

Vainly I weep my life away,—
Vainly with trembling lips I pray,
This midnight gloom might pass away.

As one, who, parched with thirst, beside
A crystal fountain's cooling tide,
Watches the bubbling waters glide,

And yet, delays to stoop and drink,
So, while I pause to doubt and think,
I perish on the river's brink.

I read the promises divine,
And see that truth and mercy shine,
Like threads of gold in every line;

But cannot feel, within my soul,
Their power to strengthen and console—
For others, I believe the whole.

I know, through all the ages past,
No contrite sinner ever cast
Himself on Christ, but found, at last,

Pardon and peace; then may not I,
Though helpless, guilty, doomed to die,
To Him, the good Physician, fly?

I will not turn to sin again,
To seek a balsam for my pain,
Though black despair for ever reign.

My soul shall cling, through deepest night,
To all that conscience owns, as right
And pleasing in my Father's sight.

I may be banished from his face;
My life for joy may find no place,
Saddest and worst of Adam's race,

But, never shall I walk again,
In godless counsels, dark and vain,
Nor in the scorner's seat remain.

When Christ, of old, on earth abode,
His heart with tender pity glowed ;
And thus the Father's love he showed.

And is he not to-day the same ?
Will he reject a sinner's claim,
That pleads his own prevailing name ?

If God is just, and man is free,
There can be no unknown decree
To crush a seeking soul, like me.

He loves the penitential tear,—
He will not turn away his ear,
From one, who comes with lowly fear.

When on my Saviour's grace I dwell,
Who died to save my soul from hell,
The tide of hope begins to swell ;

But, when I turn my eyes within,
And see my selfishness and sin,
Then Doubt and Darkness dense come in.

Shall I, o'erpowered by faithless fear,
Desponding, sit in darkness here,
Marking each vain, regretful tear ?

Although my breast's a rayless cave,
And furious foes around me rave,
I know that none but Christ can save.

To weary, burdened souls distrest,
By sin and Satan long opprest,
He offers liberty and rest.

I'll doubt no more his truth and grace,—
He loves our fallen, rebel race—
I, too, in hope, may seek his face.

Lord, at thy feet, I contrite fall,—
On thee, with trembling faith, I call,—
Save me from guilt's oppressive thrall.

Open my spirit's eyes to see
Thy power and mercy, full and free,
And let thy love encircle me.

Dawn on my heart, with healing ray—
Wash all my guilty stains away,
And turn my dreary night to day.

Father thine erring child receive—
To me the joy of sonship give,
And bid my faithless heart believe.

Then shall my soul thine image bear,—
My lips thy boundless grace declare,
And life for higher life prepare.

PART IV.—Sunrise.

The morn has broke; the night has fled,
With all its phantoms, dire and dread,
That o'er my life their shadows spread,

The Sun has risen, within my breast,
Has healed my wounds, my gloom dispersed,
And given my troubled conscience rest.

Dread forms in guilty darkness feared,
At Morning's glance have disappeared,
Or stand in radiant glory sphered.

My heart up-swells in bounding lays
Of gladness, gratitude, and praise
To Him, whose mercy crowns my days.

And can it be that I, erewhile
So faithless, sinful, dark and vile,
Bask in the sunlight of thy smile?

O mercy vast, unfathomed, free!
That lifts a worthless worm like me,
To live in fellowship with Thee.

O! that the sons of Adam knew
Thy power to quicken and renew!
Thy love, which can the heart subdue.

As one who wakes from feverish dreams,
And looks upon the tranquil beams
Of dewy morn, to whom it seems

That Earth is bathed in joy divine,
And orbs of heaven more calmly shine,
Such thoughts of rapt amaze are mine,

Since God has made his mercy known,
And Christ, the Light of Life, has shone
Within may rayless heart of stone.

As one who finds, at last, the key
To tomes of deepest mystery,
And reads, with wondering ecstacy,

Rare truths, from mortals long concealed,
Such joy, the priceless truths, revealed
To my disburdened spirit, yield.

I wonder at my disbelief,—
The weary night of fruitless grief,
Through which I vainly sought relief,

From Earth's forbidden, turbid streams,
From Folly's false misleading dreams,
And slighted Truth's enlightening beams.

The word, that holds all worlds in place,
That bids the ocean tempest cease,
To my sad heart has spoken "peace."

The ocean in its restless sway,
Bereft of every starry ray,
Can best my faithless life portray :

The ocean in its tranquil rest,
With sunbeams dancing on its breast,
My life, with peace and pardon blest.

Since Thou, Divine Redeemer, hast
Freely forgiven the guilty past,
And brought me to Thyself at last,

My ransomed powers in love receive,
Keep me from every snare, and give
The grace, that I for Thee may live.

As every glittering drop of dew
Reflects the image, clear and true,
Of the bright orb, from whom it drew

Its pearly beauty, rich and rare,
So may each thought thy likeness bear,
Each word and act thy love declare.

I know the way is rough and steep,
That storms around my head shall sweep,
But Christ, my King, shall aid and keep.

There may be wars to wage and win,
With Satan, selfishness and sin,
But He shall give me peace within.

Whatever wants my spirit knows,
Battling with self, or outward foes,
He is the Balm for all my woes.

If I am weak my King is strong,
If guilty, He forgives the wrong,
In pain, His love shall be my song.

In danger He shall be my shield,
In gloom, His presence light shall yield,
Whose word my wounded heart has healed.

A pilgrim o'er a desert wide,
If sorrows come with surging tide,
He is my Comforter and Guide.

If sick, my good Physician He,
If hungry, Bread of life for me,
If thirsty, living waters free.

My Refuge from the storms of life,—
My Captain in the battle's strife,—
My faithful Friend when foes are rife.

Though I am poor, He makes me heir
Of heavenly mansions, bright and fair,—
Unstained by sorrow sin, or care,

If problems dark perplex my brain,
Which I may try to solve in vain,
Through days and nights of fruitless pain,

I know in heaven's immortal clime,
The mists that dim the eye of Time,
No more shall shroud those truths sublime,

Which baffled human wisdom here :
Where light shall flash on every sphere,
And truth and love in all appear.

Through all my pilgrimage below,
Thy guardian care and love bestow,
And shield my soul from every woe.

And when my earthly conflicts end,
May earth with heaven serenely blend :—
Be thou my everlasting Friend.

THY KINGDOM COME.

MATT. vi: 10.

WIDE earth is fill'd with sin and sorrow,
        Enslaved by Satan's chain;
We know, full well, each fateful morrow
        Will tell its tale of pain.
Error proclaims her gilded falsehoods,
        And Truth seems strangely dumb;
Man's cruelty makes ceaseless wailing,—
        Lord, let thy kingdom come!

The souls of men, reft of thine image,
        Are homes of selfish wrong,
Where blinding and unholy passions
        Their blighting reign prolong;
Vainly they turn for hope or guidance
        To earth's distracting hum;
The heart is dark, diseased, and weary,
        Until thy kingdom come,

Millions, deep-sunk in rayless darkness,
        Thy love hath never known;
And, in their blind, misguided folly,
        Still worship wood and stone.
Dispel their darkness with thy presence,
        Call each lost wanderer home;

To every hungry soul, life-weary,
    O let thy kingdom come !

Nation with nation madly wages
    Unpitying, bloody strife,
Deeming their sordid aims more sacred
    Than peace and human life.
Earth has no medicine for these evils,
    To which all hearts succumb;
O hear our prayers, thou King immortal !
    And let thy kingdom come !

Men shut their hearts against thy mercy,
    Allured by baseless dreams;
Or use thy blessed name to strengthen
    Their godless, selfish schemes.
Thousands, who name thy name, deny thee,
    By Satan's wiles o'ercome :
Thy saints, in every land, implore thee,
    Lord, let thy kingdom come !

Tyrants still reign to crush the lowly,
    Who, wronged and injured, die ;
The woes of innocence for vengeance
    To the unceasing cry.
Come in thy peerless power and glory,
    This world from Satan win ;
Come to our hearts, all sin expelling—
    O let thy reign begin !

ONE THING IS NEEDFUL.

LUKE x: 42.

ONE thing is needful still, whatever cares
　　Absorb thy thoughts through life's unpausing
　　　　hours,
Needful alike when all around thee wears
　　The smile of joy, and when misfortune lowers.

It is not gold, that sparkles to allure,
　　Yet scorches life with selfishness and pride;
For, rich in faith and love, the lowly poor
　　May here in peace, as heirs of heaven, abide.

It is not earth's applause and empty fame,
　　So highly cherished and so madly sought;
For many a slighted and neglected name
　　Shall live, when kings and heroes are forgot.

Needful to thee above all earthly good,
　　The priceless pearl, the inner life of love
Divine; forgiveness through the sprinkled blood;
　　The joy-inspiring hope of life above.

There comes no true, soul-satisfying peace,
　　Till heaven's own love has hushed our guilty fears—
Till the wild jars of selfish passions cease,
　　And o'er our gloom the morn of joy appears.

There is no power to vanquish sin and death,—
    To work victoriously the work of heaven,—
Until the soul is linked by living faith
    To Him, by whom immortal strength is given.

No refuge can the struggling spirit find
    From pelting storms—no rest from sordid strife—
Until we flee, in trusting faith, behind
    The Rock of refuge, Christ our hope and life.

No entrance can the proudest mortal gain,
    Into the golden realms of love and joy,
Till cleansed from every guilty stain—
    Made meet by grace for heaven's divine employ.

Then seek with all thy heart, the one thing needed,
    Without which life is vain and heaven is lost;
Lest love of earth cause thee to leave unheeded
    Thy higher life—all that thy soul has cost.

DARKNESS WITHIN.

"Are the consolations of God small with thee?—is there any secret thing
with thee?"—Job xv: 11.

F in thy heart no golden sunlight lingers
  To brighten life within,
 And to the ears earth's sweet and joyous singers
  Make only doleful din :—

If, while the world is robed in perless beauty,
  Around thy spirit coil
Serpents of doubt and fear, and sacred duty
  Is heavy, joyless toil ;—

If, when thy knees are bowed in supplication,
  Struggling to cast thy care
On heaven, there comes no strength or consolation
  In answer to thy prayer ;—

Seek not to find a reason for thy sadness
  In Him who changeth not,
As if His hand witheld the light and gladness
  Which thou hast vainly sought.

All worlds upheld and gladdened by His favor,
  His boundless grace proclaim ;
Thousands rejoice in Christ, the living Saviour,
  Through changing years the same.

His loving-kindness is a fount unfailing,
    Forever full and free ;
If life is dark and prayer is unavailing,
    The hindrance is in thee.

Is there no foul impurity still clinging
    Around thy yielding heart,
Dark'ning thy inner light, and surely bringing
    This conscious guilty smart ?

Is there no idol shrined within thy spirit,
    Where God alone should reign?
No love of wrong, which gives thee to inherit
    A legacy of pain ?

Are there no works of faith and love neglected,
    To thee by Heaven assigned?
No daily Rimmon-worship, undetected,
    Blighting thy peace of mind?

Arise and search thy heart—let nothing stay thee—
    The fatal leak is there—
This traitor in thy soul may else betray thee
    To ruin and despair.

Nor doubt, when thou with heart contrite and lowly
    Hast all thy sins confest,
Thy night shall pass away, and God the holy
    Shall hear and give thee rest.

JOY-SPRINGS.

THOUGH earth is shrouded with shadows of gloom,
And life has bitter and poisoned streams,—
Though the brightest hopes are first in the tomb,
Yet Joy thickly scatters her sunny gleams.
Like stars in the night of our sunless strife,
They brighten and bless the deserts of life.

There are fountains of joy wherever we go,
Clear and deep in their silvery flow—
Wherever they sparkle in beauty's sheen,
The valleys of life wear a deeper green;
And earth has no moorland so drear and bleak,
But has beauty and joy for those who seek.

There is joy in the flush of the rosy dawn,
When the starry curtain of night is drawn,
And the earth, like a diver who sank from sight,
Emerges again from the bosom of night;
When the song of the birds, on the zephyr flung,
Gives the throbbing gladness of nature a tongue.

There is joy in the golden light of Eve,
In the gorgeous tints which the clouds receive,
Those tissues of glory of nameless dyes,

Which only gleam from the evening skies,
When mountains and vales, and lakes and streams,
Transfigured, flash in the sunset beams.

There is joy in the deeps of the silent night,
When the stars are sparkling with tremulous light,
And the vast expanse of heaven is unrolled,
Like a beautiful banner fretted with gold.
Then light-winged fancy is chained no more.
And memory opens her treasured store.

There is joy in the balmy breezes of Spring,
Which gladness and beauty around them fling,
In the bounding life of the summer hours,
With their waving fields, and their leafy bowers—
In the tranquil glory of autumn days,
When nature smiles while her pride decays:

In the chorals of hope that fall on the ear,
In life's vernal morn, soul-thrilling and clear;
In the gushing friendship which glorifies youth,
When heart beats to heart, with rapture and truth—
And joy to return, wherever we roam,
To find changeless love in the light of home.

There is speechless rapture, which none can know,
But those who have felt its magical glow,
When Nature unveils her visions of glory.
And pours on the spirit her ravishing story,

10

Which can never be breathed into mortal ears,
For it kindles emotions whose words are tears.

There is joy in the night, and joy in the day,
Joy in the autumn and joy in the spring;
Joy in the rivulet's roundelay,
Joy in the matins the wild-birds sing.
Gladness in friendship, love, and thought,
And joy in recalling bright hours forgot.

But the purest joy which the heart can know,
Doth not from an earthly fountain flow :
It comes from above, and is only given
To those who fearlessly trust in Heaven—
Who rise on the pinions of faith and love,
To drink from the fountain of life above.

A fountain that fails not in summer's blaze—
A flower which blooms through the wintry days—
Is the joy which our Father in heaven imparts,
As a balsam for weary and sorrowful hearts.
Bright amaranths bloom from an earthly sod,
For the heart that is linked by faith to its God.

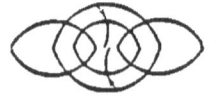

THE PRODIGAL'S RETURN.

I will arise and go to my Father, and will say unto him, Father,
I have sinned against heaven, and before thee, and am no more worthy
to be called thy son.—LUKE xv. 18, 19.

Y Father and my God,
   Prostrate before thy throne,
My base ingratitude, at last,
   With guilty shame I own:
Not worthy to behold thy face,
Or hear the accents of thy grace.

Spurning thy wise control,
   Impatient 'neath thy sway,
I've wandered, in my wayward scorn,
   Far in the downward way;
Far from my Father's home above,—
From peace, from purity, and love.

The gifts, thy grace bestowed
   To glorify thy name,
I've squandered in that far-off land,
   Nor thought from whence they came.
Life, crowned with blessings rich and free,
Has borne no fruits of love to Thee.

I bowed my neck and wore
   The yoke of Satan long,

Swept down by selfish Passion's power
    The steep descents of wrong,—
Smooth, sunny paths, which open fair,
But lead to darkness and despair.

Vainly I sought to slake
    The ceaseless thirst within,
In the impure and shallow streams
    Of carnal mirth and sin;
Nor can the husks of earth control
The hunger of the deathless soul.

Without thy love no joy
    Is found; no strength to brave
The ills and dangers dark, from which
    No arm but thine can save.
Whate'er the guilty soul may win,
There's ever want and woe within.

Madly I scorned thy love,
    And hushed my guilty fears,
And to the counsels of thy grace
    I closed my heedless ears.
I closed my eyes 'gainst truth and light
To hide the danger from my sight.

At last, with grief and pain,
    Father my guilt I see,—
I will arise, though hell oppose,
    And trusting come to Thee;

Though clothed with guilty fear and shame,
Thy heart of love is still the same.

My Father I have sinned
    Against thy wondrous grace,—
Not worthy to be called thy child,
    The lowliest servant's place
I'll take with joy, but let me be
Restored and reconciled to Thee.

My guilt no tongue tell,
    Long Satan's willing slave,
Yet hear my burdened spirit's prayer,
    My Father hear and save !
Thy life, and light, and peace impart,
And heal and cleanse my broken heart.

I hear my Father's voice,
    His lips my brow have pressed,—
His arms of love encircle me,
    And fold me to his breast;
The weary night of doubt is done,
He owns the rebel for his son.

His ring is on my hand,—
    His shoes are on my feet,—
And, robed in righteousness by faith,
    My ransom is complete :
My soul is filled with peace divine,
Joyful and rich, for God is mine.

TO A GOSPEL HERALD.

He that winneth souls is wise.—Prov. xi. 30.

F thou wouldst be a herald of thy Master,
　　Approved and owned in heaven above,
　　Let not the thought of loss or fell disaster
　　　　Outweigh thy Master's love.

Be single-eyed; fling every weight behind thee.
"Looking to Jesus" let thy race be run:
Still let His love in firm allegiance bind thee,
　　　　Till thy life-work is done.

Guard well thy heart against the subtle mentor,
　　The love of earthly praise or fame;
'Twill warp thy spirit from its living centre,
　　　　And dim thy Master's name.

For as the magnet from its pole-star veering
　　Causes the gallant ship's o'erthrow,
Shall selfish pride, at thy soul's rudder steering,
　　　　Wreck thee on reefs of woe.

When forms of wrong, which truth divine has branded
　　As heresy to God and right,
Are praised and gilded by earth's thousands, banded
　　　　To call their darkness light,

Stand firm, and drift not with the tide prevailing,—
    Still to thy King above be true :
Spare not their idol-gods, though hate and railing
        Thy Abdiel heart pursue.

Proclaim the truth, in love, with zeal unshrinking,
    Heedless of mortal praise or blame :
Among the throngs, who live and die unthinking,
        Be thou a living flame.

Though myriads lured by Fashion's syren wooing,
    At Folly's gilded altars bow,
'Gainst all that works a deathless soul's undoing,
        Firm as a rock be thou.

Still keep thy zeal by grace divine replenished—
    If living fire decline within,
Thy zeal and love for God shall be diminished—
        Thy power to vanquish sin.

Nothing but love divine can nerve thee,
    To toil with patience often tried,
For those who cannot bless or serve thee,
        But for whom Christ had died.

O'er every soul committed to thy keeping,
    Watch with a faithful shepherd's care ;
And rouse the multitudes in darkness sleeping,
        To penitence and prayer.

With erring ones be patient and forbearing,
　　Like Christ thy Master, when
He came to earth our mortal nature wearing,
　　　To save and ransom men.

He ever spoke with tenderness and favor
　　To heirs of guilt and misery :
And what wouldst thou have done, if Christ the Saviour
　　　Had not compassion'd thee?

In times when faithless, dreary darkness lowers,
　　And failure gives thy spirit pain,—
When sterile skies give neither dew nor showers
　　　To bless the scattered grain,

Be patient; wait in hope, thy labor leaving
　　In trust with Heaven. Toil on—
After the weary night of gloom and grieving
　　　Shall beam the golden dawn.

Nor murmur thou—thy work is high and holy,
　　As that of angels, bright and blest,—
To warn the erring—guide the lorn and lowly
　　　To pure and peaceful rest.

If true to God, whatever ills oppress thee.
　　When life's appointed race is run,
Thine ears shall hear the King himself address thee,
　　　"Servant of God well-done!"

SAUL ON MOUNT GILBOA.

As I happened by chance upon Mount Gilboa, behold Saul leaned upon his spear; and, lo, the chariots and horsemen followed hard after him.—2 Sam. i : 6.

E leans on his spear in his desolate grief—
His life-blood is silently streaming—
Faint, wounded, forlorn, sinks the tall Hebrew
    chief,
No hope thro' his dark bosom gleaming.

The chariots and horsemen are closing around,
And fear-stricken Israel is flying—
Their bravest and best lie strewed o'er the ground,
Where the eagle-souled chieftain is dying.

His sons in their beauty, the pride of their sire,
Repose on the battle-field gory—
No cowards, who shrinking from danger retire,—
They are crowned with the warrior's glory.

No hand near to succor as life ebbs away—
No last words of friendship to cheer him—
Of all the loved friends of life's happier day,
Not one in this dark hour is near him.

Once envied, the fame of his valor and power,
Now his star has in darkness descended—

Once the sound of his name made his enemies cower;
Now, his warfare forever is ended.

No longer by faithless ambition beguiled,
The past thrills with deepest emotion;
The thoughts that sweep o'er him are troublous and wild,
As the waves of the foam-crested ocean.

Not a star shines above to illumine or guide—
Every hope, every joy-beam is clouded—
The past is all darkened by wildering pride,
The future Despair has enshrouded.

He remembers his folly and pride with regret—
The vows he has faithlessly broken—
The dreams that in sorrow and darkness have set—
The words that should ne'er have been spoken.

The death-dealing arrows are true to their aim—
His strength and his vision are failing—
He heeds not the sound of Philistia's acclaim,
Her threats and her hate unavailing.

JESUS SHALL TAKE ME HOME.

UPON the gory battle-field
   A wounded soldier lay,
Whose thoughts were with the circle
   Beloved, though far away.
He longed to see the cherished friends,
   Of life the joy and pride,
To clasp them to his bosom
   And bless them, ere he died.

"Bring me home," he softly whispered,
   "To close my weary eye,
Where the arms of those who love me
   Shall clasp me while I die;
Let me rest beside my father,
   Where the weeping willows wave,
And the tears of holy friendship
   Shall consecrate my grave."

His brave and faithful comrade,
   With rayless grief oppressed,
Could give no hopeful answer
   To his sad and vain request;
For he struggled with a foeman,
   From whom friendship could not save;

And his eagle eye was clouded,
  With the shadows of the grave.

" The foe is closing round us,
   My life is ebbing fast;
 The day, which now is waning,
   On earth will be thy last.
 The friends who lit thy pathway
   With joy, are distant now—
 Stern death has set his signet
   Upon thy pallid brow."

Then trusting faith unfolded
  The gifts which earth denied;
While the lights of earth were fading,
  He, with joyous hope, replied:—
" Though the ties of earthly friendship,
   By death are rudely riven,
 I know the blessed Jesus
   Shall take me home to heaven."

Though scenes of gloomy terror
  And wretchedness surround,
In this sublime assurance
  Are peace and rapture found;
Though hope's gay visions vanish,
  Baseless as ocean's foam,
This thought gives light in darkness—
  " Jesus shall take me home."

Be this my chosen portion,
  Amid the toils of life;
In scenes of fear and sorrow,
  In hours of wildest strife,
To feel, though friends may fail me
  And death untimely come,
The calm and sweet assurance,
  " Jesus shall take me home."

In hours of gushing gladness,
  When life is wreathed with flowers,
The thoughtless heart may ask not
  For a fairer world than ours;
But O ! when flowers have faded,
  And wintry days draw nigh,
We need a strength and refuge
  This world cannot supply.

All earth-born bliss is transient,
  And never can control
The deep, unspoken longings,
  That beat within the soul.
The hope that shines unwaning,
  When life's bright spring has flown—
The joy that blooms forever,
  Is found in God alone.

THE DEPARTING YEAR.

I.

HE funeral knell of the dying Year
Is softly rung by the midnight Hour,
And mournfully falls on the wakeful ear,
Thrilling the soul with its mystic power.
It comes like the voices of Earth and Time,
Re-echoed back from the deeps sublime
Of the spirit world beyond the tomb,
Which Fate has shrouded in starless gloom.
This farewell knell has vividly brought
To my pensive heart the thrilling thought,
That the Year, that has swiftly and silently flown,
Has borne away to Jehovah's throne
A record of all it has witnessed on earth,
Of evil and good since the hour of its birth.
The crimes that blacken the life are there,
Beside the deeds of mercy and prayer.

II.

Old Year, though thy life swept swiftly by,
Strange visions have past 'neath thy sleepless eye;
Thou hast watched while brothers have met in fight,
On fields where thousands were ruthlessly slain,
And thousands more through the dreary night
Lay writhing unfriended, in deathly pain.

Thou hast heard the merry bridal bells
Peal out, with jubilant gleesome swells;
And heard them toll on the funeral day,
As the beautiful bride was laid in the clay.

III.

Thou hast seen the waving flowers of hope
Bloom under a brilliant and cloudless cope,
When beautiful birds sang in vernal bowers,
By sparkling streams; and the golden hours
Ever bore on their swift and silent wings
Such joy-dreams as Hope to Fancy brings,
Till blight and decay came over the scene,
And nothing remained of joys that had been;
For all, that was bright and beautiful there,
Lies under the wintry snows of despair.

IV.

Within thy brief and shadowy reign,
What sorrows of poverty, falsehood and pain—
What visions of gladness that never came—
Of riches—of love—and deathless fame—
Have vanished, and left not a trace to show,
That ever hath been either joy or woe!
The castles which Fancy had built on the sand
Were effaced by thy swift invisible hand,
And the dreaded ills of thy natal day,
Like phantoms of night have glided away.
Thou hast heard the vows which the sufferer's lips
So ardently breathed, in Sorrow's eclipse,
And sadly saw, when the storm passed o'er,
That his passionate vows were remembered no more.

V.

I recall the bygone Year with regret,—
The stars of hope that forever have set,—
The dreams of achievement that never were won,
And deeds of promise that still are undone,—
The battles with Doubt and Passion fought—
The lessons which Sorrow and Darkness taught—
The pictures of beauty which nature spread—
The friends that have sunk to sleep with the dead—
The joy that flashed like the morning light,
When Truth spread her starry gems to my sight—
The faithlessness, folly, and selfish pride,
Which bygone days in their darkness hide—
Like spectral shadows they haunt me yet,
Beclouding this hour with gloom and regret.

VI.

The muffled tread of departing Years,
As they pass with their burden of gladness and tears,
Mournfully whispers of change and decay—
The fairest and best are passing away—
And wakes in my sad and yearning breast
A longing for pure and tranquil rest—
A home where the flowers shall ever bloom,
And life never feel the blight of the tomb;
Where decay and grief shall forever cease,
And no selfish sorrow shall jar my peace;
Where the power of sin and death shall be past,
And love and joy shall eternally last.

Songs of Home and Heart.

OUR LITTLE BOY.

WHEN October had stript the trees
    Of their gorgeous crimson and gold,
  And the moan of the sorrowful breeze
    The desolate Winter foretold,
  A cherub boy to our household came—
    Like a beam of golden light
Sent down from the world, where life is love,
  To brighten life's wintry night.

Our Sunbeam has opened new mines of love,
  Whose wealth was unknown before;
He has kindled a light in home and heart,
  That shall burn till life is o'er.
As we softly bend o'er his placid sleep,
  To imprint a kiss on his brow,—
How little he knows of the watch we keep,
  And the love that encircles him now!

Every tiny form and childish voice
  Brings our little boy to mind—
He has made my heart to those opening flowers
  More thoughtfully, tenderly kind.

11

I hear the patter of little feet
  With emotions before unknown—
To our joy-lit hearts the world seems changed,
  Since baby has taken his throne.
Every playful trick of childish glee
  Has a charm for our wondering eyes;
And even his prattling, broken speech
  Seems quaint, and wondrously wise.
His eye is bright, and his voice is sweet
  As a wood-bird's matin hymn—
We feel in our silent, grateful joy,
  That there never was child like him.

And yet, in the flush of my joy and pride,
  I am thrilled with a painful emotion,
As I wistfully glance along life's tide,
  Toward eternity's boundless ocean.
O! what if the ruthless angel of death,
  Should steal in some fatal hour,
And blight with his terrible, icy breath
  Our precious and beautiful flower!

The thought of a fate so darkly drear,
  Comes piercing with arrows of pain;
Eclipsing with shadows of murky fear
  The hopes that have haunted my brain.
If the cherub whose love gives rare delight,
  To the land of the dead should flee,
The dreary shades of a starless night
  Would darken the world to me.

But worse than death is the bitter cup,
  That is pressed to a parent's lips,
When the light of purity, peace and hope,
  Is quenched in a dark eclipse ;
For blight may fall on the fairest flowers—
  Life has many a hidden snare—
And hopes, that have risen as brightly as ours,
  Have set in the gloom of despair.

I often muse on his future fate,
  And picture what it may be,
Till darkness comes down on my musing soul,
  Like night on a surging sea.
O! which shall he choose ere youth has flown,
  The path of sorrow or joy ?
And if I should fall and leave him alone,
  Who would watch o'er my fatherless boy ?

Father in heaven! our orisons hear,
  And shield him from sin and from harm—
May our love be tempered with wisdom and fear—
  And our strength be thy holy arm :
May the feet of our darling never stray
  In the paths of folly and woe,
May he choose the pleasures that never decay,
  Above all that sparkles below.

If father and mother should droop and die,
  And sorrowful fortune portend,

Be Thou his defence when danger is nigh,
   A pity Father and Friend.
Be Thou his Guide through life's perilous way,
   Till temptation and conflict are past;
And, wherever o'er earth his feet may stray,
   Bring him home to Thyself at last.

—⁘⁘⁘—

A SONNET.

WRITTEN IN SICKNESS.

FRAGILE and brittle, as a glassy urn,
   Is this frail casket which our life contains;
   A breath may wring it with most poignant pains
   And aches.   A rude unkindly touch may turn
Our strength to feebleness, our hopes to dust.
   'Tis hard, amid our dreams, our active strife
With stern, unfriendly Fate, to feel we must
   Renounce each task, that gave sweet zest to life,
And like a bird whose wing in flight is broken,
   Or fleet-winged yacht, disabled in the race,
Can only wait, and watch with thoughts unspoken
   Those happier souls, who near the goal apace:
Yet he who calmly waits when clouds o'ercast
His life, may gain the richest prize at last.

A FATHER'S FAREWELL.

O my son, I will no longer
With my selfish love detain,
Dreams of hope and fame are round thee,
Voices from life's distant main.
Out on life's broad, billowy ocean
Richer prizes may be won,
We have only love to give thee—
Stay not longer here my son.

Happy days! now gone forever,
When I watched thy opening mind,
Listened to thy childish fancies,
In thy playful frolics joined:
Then, I often wished the older,
Now, I wish the young again;
For the dark uncertain future
Flings its shadows o'er my brain.

I have watched thy young ambition
Throbbing for a higher sphere—
Broader streams of truth and beauty,
Than could quench thy longing here;
And around my heart those shadows
Have for years in silence grown,

As I saw this hour approaching—
Hour that leaves me sad and lone.

Though thy love be true and constant,
Till the years of life are o'er,
Some prophetic feeling tells me
That my son is mine no more.
And when distant every object,—
Every hill and every tree,
With a mute and mournful language,
To my heart shall speak of thee.

Not till round thy knees, in beauty,
Fairy forms shall softly rise,
And a father's wordless feeling
Glistens in thy dewy eyes,
Canst thou know the love and sadness,
Which my heaving bosom swell,—
For no words of mine can tell thee
All that burdens this farewell.

When the fleeting years have brought thee
All thy youthful dreams portrayed,—
And, new hopes, new joys, and friendships,
At thy feet in tribute laid,
Then forget not those who loved thee,
Ere the world had known thy name,
With a love more rare and precious,
Than the choicest gifts of fame.

Wintry days may yet befall thee,
Hours of conflict try thy soul,—
And, around thy storm-swept spirit,
Fierce and furious billows roll ;
But, whatever change comes o'er thee,
Sternly, nobly act thy part ;
And, when darkest ills assail thee,
Faith will stay thy faltering heart.

Let not selfish passion blind thee,
Wrong to act, or false to speak—
Know, whatever fate betide thee,
Truth is strong and falsehold weak.
Still, the eyes of God the holy
Every thought and deed behold,
And a pure and peaceful conscience
Never can be bought with gold.

Day and night my prayers shall bless thee,
Till my beating heart shall cease—
May thy false and guilty folly
Never blight a father's peace.
In the dim and distant future,
Fame and friendship may be thine ;
But this world can never give thee
Deeper, truer love than mine.

THE ORPHAN.

T his birth, there were gushes of grateful joy,—
    A mother's love and a father's pride
Were blended to welcome a beautiful boy—
    A waif on life's treacherous tide.
A flower in a sheltered nook he grew,
    Secure when the chill winds were rife :
The genial light and the silver dew
    Kindly nourished its dawning life.

How tenderly watched, with loving eyes,
    What visions of gladness, to hope appears
To rise and bloom, 'neath the genial skies
    Of the joy-laden coming years,
Is only known to the Father above,
    Whose goodness immensity fills,—
Who has given such wealth of deathless love
    To soften life's darkling ills.

But the father, so hopeful, true, and brave—
    The mother, so tenderly loving and kind,
Together have sunk to an early grave,
    And left him unfriended behind.

He never can hear a mother's voice,
    Nor pillow his head on her breast;
She shall never again sing the songs of his choice,
    That so often have lulled him to rest.

Now, fatherless, motherless, sad and lone,
    His path is thorny and steep;
For the golden days have forever flown,
    Ere sorrow had taught to weep.
There is none to love, or care for him now—
    To hearten when sad and opprest—
The light has faded from his young brow,
    And the joy of hope from his breast.

A hireling lad, he earns his bread
    Sadly toiling each grinding day;
The sunlight of joy is never shed
    To brighten his cheerless way.
His face is tann'd with the sun and wind,—
    His garments are coarse and thin;
But worse, for the lack of love, his mind
    Grows stolid and coarse within.

Not a friend for his bitterest woe to feel—
    Alone he must buffet the wave—
The heart that would ache for his grief is still,
    In the dark and pitiless grave.
None cares for the friendless, fatherless boy,—
    No need to be gentle or just,—

The arm that would shield him from wrong with joy,
　　Is lifeless and low in the dust.

Ah! many a mother, whose budding flowers
　　Are cherished, than rubies more,
Would weep sad tears through life's sunniest hours,
　　Could she see the sorrow in store,—
The deadly battles with Want and Fear,
　　The freezing blasts of a wintry sky,
That shall darken the lot of her children dear,
　　Unseen by a mother's eye.

And yet there is One, to whose sleepless eye
　　All unkindness and wrong are known,
Who hears the poor and the helpless cry,
　　And counts their wrongs as his own.
And he that injures the fatherless boy
　　Shall his selfishness vainly deplore,
When sorrow gives place to eternal joy,
　　And the orphan is orphan no more.

A MOTHER'S LAMENT.

SHE came, a bright and beauteous thing,
    When bird-songs fill'd the listening air,
    When buds and flowers were rich and fair,
Herself the fairest flower of spring.

A sunbeam from the starry clime—
    A blossom from the dewy skies,
    That softly oped its violet eyes,
To beautify life's vernal prime.

She kindled in my heart the while
    A glow of rapture, pure as gold—
    A world of happiness untold
Was dimpled in her winsome smile.

Sweetly she grew in love's soft light,
    Till thought shone out with witching grace,
    From her blue eyes and sunny face,
And flung a radiance o'er our night.

Like clinging vine around the oak,
    Twining around our hearts she grew,
    With love so silent, warm and true,
By its untwining hearts are broke.

Like dew-drop in a rose-bud shrined,
  Which, while it shines, new life imparts,
  She softly nestled in our hearts,
And with her beauty life refined.

But, when her prattling infant tongue
  Worded in speech her budding thought,
  Like witching music, zephyr-brought,
Her soft and silvery accents rung.

The warbled song of forest bird,
  The rarest notes of lute or lyre,
  The melodies of chanting choir,
Were never with such rapture heard.

Ah! many an hour of silent joy
  I spent, in visions golden-hued,
  Of joys which Fancy richly strew'd
Around her life, as Love's own dower.

I saw her in her maiden pride,
  A blossom beautifully fair,
  All robed in vestments rich and rare,
A worthy lover's peerless bride.

My golden dreams were rudely broken—
  A blight fell on my budding rose—
  Its opening leaves forever close,—
A grief that never can be spoken.

We watched her slow, but sure decay;
    From her blue eyes the light departed;
    And left us, lone and broken-hearted,
Like wither'd leaves on wintry spray.

She, whom I thought, when life declined,
    Would watch with love my failing breath,
    And close my weary eyes in death,
Has left me desolate behind.

Her loss has darkenèd all the spheres—
    Covered life's golden hopes with rust—
    Vainly I now bedew her dust,
With Sorrow's bitter, briny tears.

As one who drops, in some dark nook,
    A precious pearl, long vainly sought,
    Can never pass the luckless spot,
Without a vain regretful look;

So this sequestered, greening mound,
    Where sleeps her dust in still repose,
    Recalls my withered, budding rose.
Old mother, Earth seems holy ground,

Since she has sheltered in her breast,
    My precious flower, forever dear:
    It seems so far from earth, the sphere,
Where our departed idols rest.

A bird that sings, while skies are clear,
　　Sweet songs in leafy forest-bowers,
　　And cheers and charms the sunny hours,
Till wintry storms and gloom draw near;

A snowflake from its home on high,
　　Which sinks to earth awhile;
　　Then, drawn by heaven's transforming smile,
Rises and seeks its native sky;—

Awhile she sang our cares to sleep—
　　Awhile our snowflake shone below;
　　But she has fled, and none can know
How deep the shades in which we weep.

At times, in lonely musing rapt,
　　My angel-child seems hovering near;
　　The rustle of her wings I hear,
She smiles, as ere life's cord was snapt.

Or, in my radiant happy dreams,
　　She comes from heaven, a welcome guest,
　　I clasp her fondly to breast,
My waking woe a fancy seems;

Then I awake and all is night,
　　More deep and rayless than before;
　　I think my weary thinkings o'er,
Till dawns the blessed morning light.

The world is robed in joy no more ;
    The stars shine not as once they shone ;
    Each bird-song has a plaintive tone ;
And life has lost the light of yore.

But from this bitter root, in tears
    And darkness planted, yet may bloom
    Flowers that shall brighten her lone tomb,
And scatter fragrance o'er the years.

Since my life's idol has been broken,
    My heart shall seek its gladness now,
    From Him alone to whom I bow,
And own His stroke as love's dark token.

While here, by Care's unresting strife,
    Rudely and sorrowfully riven,
    My hopes, my joys are all in heaven,
The land of shadeless love and life.

MY STUDY.

THIS is a sacred spot—a cherished place
To me.   Although to other eyes appear
No charm or beauty—no sculptor's art to grace,—
No painter's skill with beauteous forms to cheer
Its solitude.—Yet all my wealth is here.
   Memory shall gather up each gem with care,
Within her casket, as a treasure dear ;
And hither Fancy shall betimes repair—
A spot where Hope has often battled with Despair.

Here have I oft from low-born cares retired,
To hold communion with the starry dead,
Whose deathless deeds and lofty thoughts inspired
My youthful soul, and hopeful purpose fed.
Oft as in thought they past with regal tread,
I longed to follow in the paths they trod,
To work in hope till life's last evening fled,
That when my dust should sleep beneath the sod,
The deathless self might rise to reign with God.

As some slight fissure in the time-worn rocks
May open into caverns deep and wide,
Where endless passages, with creeks and lochs
And wondrous sights, in sunless darkness hide ;

So this small room to me has oft supplied
A gateway to a new and boundless clime,
Where, led by some immortal guide,
I have with joy explored those streams sublime,
Whose waters fertilize and bless the fields of time.

What transport in my kindled bosom sprang,
As fancy wandered through long-vanished years,
HOMER and MILTON in their blindness sang,—
SHAKESPEARE provoked to laughter or to tears;
Now LUTHER thunders truths which Leo fears;
BACON shines forth the courtier and the sage;
BUNYAN portrays a pilgrimage of tears;
WESLEY rebukes the errors of his age;
Or FOX and CHATHAM write their names on England's
      page.

Now toils philosophy, with torch reared high,
To chase the shadows which perplex the brain;
Or science opens to the wondering eye
The secret forces earth and air contain,—
The changeless laws by which they each attain
Their end.   Or else to beauty's realms depart,
Where poetry unveils her glorious reign,
Interprets nature with mysterious art,
Or, with a touch, lays bear the human heart.

But, chief of all, the Book of books has here
Opened its treasures to the hungry mind,

Shed on my darkness gleams of light sincere,
Pictures of truth and purity, refined
From the foul mists of sin, which shroud and blind
The selfish hearts of men.   In Christ I see,
Unveiled to mortal sight, the love, and kind
Compassion of my Father's heart to me,
And hear His voice of truth and mercy, full and free.

Here have I struggled in pursuit of truth
With eager search, as for the morning light
The watcher looks; and felt the joy of youth,
When some rich pearl has sparkled to my sight.
And here, when all were wrapt in dreams of night,
Have glorious visions floated thro' my brain,
Which filled my being with serene delight,
Quickened the pulse of gladness, silenced pain,
And thrilled my soul like some celestial harper's strain.

Here, too, in hours of darkness and despair,
When my sad spirit sank by grief opprest
And torn, I've bowed in troubled, anxious prayer,
And sought, for all the anguish of my breast,
Relief from Him who gives the weary rest;
Till the freed spirit rose on eagle wings
Of joy, no more by guilt and fear distrest ;
Triumphant faith her heavenly anthems sings,
And over life's dark glades, immortal radiance flings.

Let others choose the pleasure-seeking throng,

Where gilded splendors charm the thoughtless eye ;
Where, 'mid the voice of revelry and song,
Thousands forget that living men must die.
For such delights I will not breathe a sigh,
While here most choice companionship I find
With all the great and good, who time defy :
Here peaceful hours, by holy thoughts refined,
Shall nerve, and plume for loftier flight the deathless
mind.

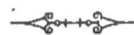

SNOW-FLAKES.

SOFTLY the fragile ermine snow-flakes fall :
From the dim cloud-land of their airy birth,
They come to shroud the naked, shivering earth,
Like Heaven's vast love, which crowns and covers
all.
They whirl and dance through all the frosty air—
On lakes and rivers fall and melt unseen ;
Each branching spray receives an ample share,
Till woods are fairer than in summer green.
They crown the trees with graceful plumes of light,
Deck hills and vales in robes of peerless beauty,
Smooth every rugged spot, as if their duty
Was to remove deformity from sight,
And spread an emblem o'er this dark terrene
Of stainless purity and peace serene.

A CHRISTMAS CAROL.

AKE the tide of cheerful song,
  Loud and gladsome anthems sing;
Round the flashing fireside throng,
  Let each home with gladness ring.
Children round, where'er ye roam,
  Check your wayward steps awhile;
Bless your early childhood's home,
  With the sunlight of your smile.
Happy parents greet to-day
Wanderers from the far-away.

Glad the mother clasps her boy,
  Wondering at his manly form;
And the tide of houschould joy
  Rises higher than the storm.
Merry sleigh-bells fill the air—
Youths and maidens gliding' past—
Sounds of gladness everywhere
  Mingle with the wintry blast.
Pile the blazing maple higher,
Joy to-day bids Care retire.

Yet, while all around is gay,
Many a mother's pensive thought
Follows one that's far away,

Till the mirth is all forgot.
To the wanderer, who strays
Far from home and friends of youth,
Comes the memory of the days,
Bright with hopeful love and truth;
And a silent tear is shed
Over hopes, forever fled.

Many a home is lone and drear,
Which last Christmas-tide was glad;
And a father's empty chair
Tells why every heart is sad.
Or perhaps the darling child,
Who, a year ago to-day,
Lightly tripped and gaily smiled,
Joined in all the merry play,
Sleeps, with cold and pulseless breast,
Where the weary are at rest.

Many a weary child of sorrow,
Who can scarce his burden bear,
Trembling at each dark to-morrow,
Friendless, joyless, torn with care,
Wins to-day a brief release
From the weary, grinding strife,—
Gains a sunny hour of peace,
Such as rarely brightens life;
And a glimpse of heaven's rest
Flickers through his toil-worn breast.

Ye whom kindly heaven has blest,
And who want have never known,
Never burdened or opprest,
Left to weep in grief alone,—
Many a bleak and sunless spot,
Where unbroken winter reigns,
By the selfish world forgot,
Crushed and bleeding hearts contains;
And it may be yours to throw
Gleams of sunshine o'er their woe.

'Mid our happy, thoughtless play,
Let us pause to ask the reason
Why we keep this Christmas-day,
As a happy, joyous season :
Ever gladly keep in mind
How the love of heaven was shown,
When the Saviour, meek and kind,
Looked from glory's brightest throne—
Saw our world in woe and sin—
Swiftly came to save and win.

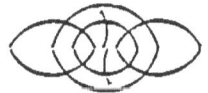

A FOREST FUNERAL.

THEY crossed the deep, with a hopeful breast,
   From the land of their love and pride,
To find a home in the glorious West,
   Where Freedom and Peace abide.
With Sorrow and Hope waging equal strife,
   They left Erin's emerald shore;
And the toilsome years of their rugged life
   Long bravely and patiently bore.

In the shades of the vast Canadian wood,
   Far away from the dwellings of pride,
The humble and lonely shanty stood,
   Where their darling faded and died.
She had been the joy of their lonely lot,
   A playful and beautiful child,
Whose winning prattle and budding thought
   Had brightened their solitude wild.

In rayless sorrow the mother weeps;
   Her heart is wounded and sore—
And she thinks of a blighted blossom, that sleeps
   In death on her natal shore.
She recalls the friends that were tried and true,
   That no longer can soothe or cheer—

The happy home which her girlhood knew,
    And she vainly wishes them near.

" O why did I ever so thoughtlessly leave
    My home in the sea-circled isle,
To come to a land where I vainly grieve
    For sympathy's tear or smile ?
For our life at best is fleeting and brief,
    A few short sorrowful years "—
Thus she wildly wails, till her bitter grief
    Is tempered by friendly tears.

The father's step is heavy and slow—
    Vainly hiding his inward smart,
The strong man bending 'neath Sorrow's blow,
    Is a grief that pierces the heart.
He knew he would miss, for many a day,
    The musical voice of his pet—
The charms that kept Care and Sadness at bay,
    And silenced the voice of Regret.

And the children sadly and tenderly came
    To the cot, where the innocent lay,
To weep o'er the statue-like, waxen flame,
    Ere they laid it to rest in the clay.
No coffin prepared with costly art,
    For the little sleeper arrayed—
By the father's hand, with a bleeding heart,
    Its last little crib was made.

No words could their desolate anguish speak,
    As they bore their treasure away,
In the lonely depths of the woods to seek
    The grave where another lay.
So deep is the yearning for friendship shown
    Alike by the timid and brave,
That we seek when the light of life has flown
    For fellowship in the grave.

The blighted rose-bud to life so dear,
    The father tenderly bore—
How vain will the pageants of earth appear,
    When the dreams of this world are o'er !
Their trackless way was rugged and long —
    Their words were broken and brief,
And the birds seem'd to warble a plaintive song,
    As if they were touched with grief.

Oe'r the creek, that was bridged by a fallen tree,
    Through swamp and thicket they passed ;
Till under a wide-spreading beech they see
    The grave which they sought, at last.
No priest was there with pretentious form
    To hallow the virgin sod ;
But honest hearts, with affection warm,
    Surrendered her back to God.

They laid her low in the beech-tree's.shade,
    While silent and sorrowful prayer

Arose to God, that his love might aid
   This burden of woe to bear—
The man of stern and simple faith,
   And he who counted his beads;
For the wail of Sorrow—the stroke of Death—
   Can silence the jar of creeds.

Deep grief can the selfish heart unseal,
   And kindlier thoughts impart,
And wake the torpid spirit to feel
   For the woes of a fellow heart.
Like stars that rise when the sun has set,
   Love shines in the night of grief;
With soothing words of kind regret,
   Bringing wounded hearts relief.

Back through the deep-shaded woods they come,
   More lone than they felt before,
For a light had gone out in their forest home,
   That could never be kindled more.
And long the shadow of death o'erhung
   Their life, as they listened in vain,
For the bounding foot and the silvery tongue,
   That they never shall hear again.

That forest grave is by all forgot—
   Not a grassy mound appears—

Not a stone points out that sacred spot,
    Once hallowed by passionate tears :
And yet, when I yield this fleeting breath,
    I ask not a costlier tomb—
Let me sleep the tranquil sleep of death,
    Where the flowers of the forest bloom.

STORM AT MIDNIGHT.

Hear to-night the weird and lonely wail
    Of broad Ontario's storm-swept moaning waves ;
    Along the shore the tempest wildly raves ;
The winds are burdened with a doleful tale.
Beneath a scowling sky the snows are driven,
    Madly defiant of each genial law.
To such an hour mysterious power is given
    To thrill the soul with vague and speechless awe ;
As if on wings of darkness through the hoarse
    And lonesome air, beyond the sphere of life,
Fierce spirit-messengers, with furious force,
    Were hurrying on to join in some dread strife,
On which results of deathless fate depend,
Beyond what mortal thought can comprehend.

OUR DEAD.

DIED—On Christmas-day, Wilhelmina, youngest child of Mr. B—.
G—, aged four years and four months.—*Country paper.*

WHILE Christmas bells were gaily ringing
    Their chimes of gladsome praise,
To many a heart unbidden bringing
    The joys of other days,

Death swooped from his cloud-hidden eyrie,
    And snatch'd from love's embrace
The budding-flower—the household fairy—
    In childhood's winsome grace.

No time too sacred for his visit—
    No form too fair can be—
Does he exult in pain, or is it
    Wisdom we cannot see?

In the bright dawn of youthful beauty—
    In age and frail decay—
In the stern strife of toil and duty,
    Our joy-stars fade away.

Yet may we find some healing token
    Of wisdom love or truth,

Whether the cord of life be broken
In age or bounding youth.

Mourn not for those whom Christ has folded,
    Safe from earth's weary strife;
Tis ours by conflict to be moulded—
    Theirs to inherit life.

They are not lost—they pass before us;
    They set in heaven to rise:
Their memory softly beameth o'er us,
    Like stars in wintry skies.

Their words by love are shrined and sainted—
    Their deeds forever dear.
Their forms, by memory deftly painted,
    Seem often sweetly near.

Weep not the young, who early dying,
    Are saved from countless woes;
They never see the pain and sighing
    Which lengthened years disclose.

The plants too frail for earthly garden,
    In heaven's bright balmy air
Where Love is Joy's unsleeping warden,
    Shall golden fruitage bear.

Weep not for those, who, old and hoary
    Sink calmly to their rest,

As clouds all steep'd in sunset glory
   Sink on the ocean's breast.

Nor yet for those whom Death has smitten
   In manhood's strength and pride ;
Their names upon our hearts are written,
   Who in stern battle died.

Our love for those whom God has taken
   Is cleansed from selfish stains ;
By time undimm'd, by storms unshaken,
   Still pure and strong remains.

Thus, one by one, the gentle-hearted,
   Whose love with ours entwined,
Have to the land of life departed,
   And left us lone behind.

When darkly fall the shades of even,
   It gives us joy to know
We have more friends beloved in heaven,
   Than earth retains below.

Their love like golden chains shall bind us
   To those immortal bowers,
In which they rest, till Death remind us
   That heaven is also ours.

National and Patriotic Pieces.

ODE TO CANADA.

GOD bless our noble Canada!
  Our broad and free Dominion!
Where law and liberty have sway,—
Not one of all her sons to-day
  Is tyrant's serf or minion.

Give joy a tongue, let peaceful mirth
  Dispel all faithless fears—
We hail a youthful nation's birth,
Who, in the wondering eyes of Earth,
  Takes rank among her peers.

Fling out our banner to the breeze,
  And proudly greet the world
With words of amity and peace;
For never on more halcyon seas
  Was Freedom's flag unfurled.

Thrice hail! our own beloved land!
  By God to freemen given:
We seek no distant golden strand,—
No other home shall we demand,
  Till home we find in heaven.

We boast no charms of high degree
  In wealth, in rank, or blood.
No tales of knightly chivalry—
Long lines of lordly ancestry—
  Nor haunted stream or wood.

No proud historic names have we,
  Whose memory thrills the heart—
No scenes embalmed by Poesie—
No hoary castles grand to see—
  The pride of ancient art.

But though the past has records few
  Of battle, song, or story,
The Future rises fair to view,
Gleaming with morning's youthful dew,
  And bright with coming glory.

O fair and fertile Canada !
  Where thought and speech are free,
Where'er my roaming feet may stray—
Whatever fate may come—I pray
  That God may shelter thee.

Thy forests grand to wander through,
  Still as in youth I love—
Thy trees, thy flowers of varied hue—
I love thy glorious lakes, as blue
  And vast as heaven above.

I love thy green and towering hills—
    Thy valleys rich and fair,
Where wealth in pearly dew distils—
Thy cool meandering forest rills,
    Hid from the summer glare.

I love thy rivers broad and free—
    Thy cataracts sublime,
Where God unveils his majesty—
Whose hymns make grandest melody,
    That strikes the ear of Time.

I love thy bright and balmy Spring—
    Thy leafy Summer bowers,
Where gay thy woodland songsters sing,
And every zephyr's airy wing
    Is redolent of flowers.

I love when Autumn's brilliant dyes
    Thy forest foliage stain,
And Nature yields her rich supplies—
I love when Winter's ermine lies
    On river, wood and plain.

I love thy homes whose light retains,
    Brave sons and daughters fair,
Where liberty with truth remains,
And every loyal heart disdains
    A servile yoke to wear.
    13

And all that England boasts we claim
  By right which none denies—
Her valor and undying fame—
Each noble deed and kingly name,
  That o'er oblivion rise.

The rich inheritance of thought,
  Which golden fruitage bears—
Achievements hero-hearts have wrought—
Freedom by bloody battles bought—
  Are ours as well as theirs.

Our fathers fought on gory plains
  To vanquish Albion's foes ;
And, though between us ocean reigns,
We are no aliens—in our veins
  The blood of Britain flows.

Land of the river, lake, and wood—
  Of loving hearts and true—
Fair child of Parent great and good—
While joined in loyal brotherhood,
  No foe can us subdue.

If ever foeman's hostile tread
  Should stain Canadian strand,
Our enemies shall learn with dread,
How freely will our blood be shed
  To guard our native land.

ERIN REMEMBERED.

FAIR Canada, land of the maple and pine,
    Though liberty, grandeur and beauty are thine,
    Yet in sweet, dreamy sadness my thoughts often
        roam,
    To re-visit loved Erin, my country—my home !

Though the wide-ocean parts from that beautiful isle,
Yet memory and fancy oft sweetly beguile,
And bear me on pinions of rapture, to gaze
On the scenes where I sported, in youth's sunny days.

While the shadows of twilight sink down on the hills,
And the moan of the pine-trees with tenderness thrills,
On this old mossy log I recline with delight,
And dream of a spring-time, long faded from sight.

The song of the lark, so hopeful and clear,
And nature's wild minstrelsy, sweeter than art,
Float over the deep to my solitude here,
And kindle the smouldering fires at my heart.

Hibernia, my birth-land, though dark o'er thy brow
Fall shadows of sorrow and poverty now,
Like a vision of beauty thine image I view,
An emerald set in the measureless blue.

I often re-visit thee, Erin, in dreams ;
And wander, with joy, by thy lochs and thy streams ;
Through thy meadows, where daisies and primroses gay
Begem with their glory the beautiful May.

Thy heathery mountains are hoary and grand—
Thy valleys as fair as the heart can demand—
Thy fields ever green, in the freshness of youth,
And the hearts of thy children with friendship and truth.

I remember the home, where in childhood I played—
I remember the hills, where in boyhood I strayed—
I remember, with shadows of sorrow and pain,
The friends, that I never can meet with again.

My father, revered, is long cold in the clay—
My mother, beloved, calmly sleeps by his side—
My brothers and sisters all faded away—
Ere the bloom of the spring-time had vanished, they died.

The land where I live wears the blossoms of hope,
No clouds charged with sorrow yet darken her cope ;
In the land to which memory so tenderly turns,
There is only the ashes of joy in her urns.

I shall never return to my fatherland now—
Time has whitened the locks on my care-wrinkled brow—
Though still dear to my heart, the land o'er the sea
Is no longer a home and a country to me.

THE CAPTURE OF QUEBEC.

 Hundred years have glided past, thick-starred with
  deeds renowned,
Since mingled French and British blood crimsoned
  Canadian ground,
September came with peaceful mien, and Nature
  look'd as fair
As if the bloody strife of war could never taint her air.
Secure in proud defiant strength, Quebec sits on the height ;
Her children gaily laugh to scorn old England's boasted might ;
Their walls are strong—their cliffs are steep—their warriors
  brave and true—
'Tis vain to fear ; no mortal foe can vanquish or subdue.

The broad St. Lawrence sweeps along, with silent chainless
  power ;
The fisher sings his vesper song, the maid sings in her bower :
It is a brooding solemn eve, as if the coming strife
Had cast its shadow o'er the world, and hush'd its bounding
  life.
The city, on her rocky height, flash'd in the setting sun,
Till Day folds up his wings of light, and Labor's task is done.
Awhile the moon, with tranquil light, silver'd the antique town,
Then in the river's bosom sank, and ebon gloom came down.
Slowly and silently, beneath the sheltering wings of Night,
The British floated down the tide and scaled the craggy height,

Till ere the eye of Dawn had pierced the gloom, or Day was
    born,
Drawn up in stern array they stood, and waited for the morn.
There comrade promised comrade, while waiting for the light,
If on the coming day one should perish in the fight,
He, who survived the fate of war, should o'er the ocean wave
Bear the last word and token his dying comrade gave.

Ah many a gallant heart, that burns with hope and dauntless
    pride,
Or sadly thinks of kindred dear, beyond the Atlantic wide,
Before to-morrow's sun has set shall sleep in death's dark sleep.
While nations wonder at the deeds, which fame shall proudly
    · keep.
The sturdy sons of Albion's soil, firm as the granite rock,
Who never falter or recoil in battle's fiercest shock—·
The sons of Erin, bold and free, whose life-blood has been shed
Wherever Britain's honored flag has floated o'er her dead—

The hardy Highlanders whose fame all climes and countries
    know,
Who never in the wildest strife turned back to mortal foe—
To these a captain has been given, unquailing, gen'rous, brave,
As ever led the van of war on battle-field or wave.
A scout to Montcalm brought the word, that in the dead of
    night
The English host had scaled the steep, and now were on the
    height—

" They shall not long remain," he said, " beneath our city
    walls ;
Now Frenchmen, on to meet the foe, 'tis France and honor
    calls."

Not long the eager French delay to close in fierce attack ;
They swept with fiery valor on to drive the English back ;
A moment face to face they stood, and then in conflict close ;
But seldom on the field of fame have met such gallant foes.
The thin, red line awaiting them received the furious shock,
As break the surging billows wild, upon the ocean rock.
Now Britons, by your country's fame, her honor and renown,
By all the sacred memories which by-gone ages crown,
By priceless love and friendship, unchanged in weal or woe,
Stand firm and quit you valiantly, ye have a worthy foe.
Sternly they waged the deadly strife, bravely they fought and
    well,
While many a youthful warrior, and fameless hero fell :
Wherever raged the wildest strife, and conflict was most keen,
Leading his dauntless comrades on, the form of WOLFE was
    seen.
With equal valor Montcalm led the chivalry of France—
But vain are all their valiant deeds—their daring foes
    advance !

At length the British chieftain gave forth the stern command
To charge upon the Frenchmen, with bayonet in hand,—
Thro' showers of fiery hail the red-cross flag they bore,
Nor quailed when death and danger grew deadlier than before !

No power on earth could long withstand that line of gleaming
    steel ;
Before the hurricane of death the broken Frenchmen reel ;
The gallant MONTCALM sank in death, ere yet his comrades
    fled—
Rather than bear defeat, he chose to sleep among the dead.

And WOLFE, the peerless and the brave, by England loved so
    well,
Maintained her honor with his life—in victory's arms he fell.
" They run ! they run ! " the welcome sound rang on the
    startled air.
He heard the thrilling words—thanked Heaven—and died
    victorious there.
MONTCALM and WOLFE shall ever grace Canadian song and
    story ;
Both with their life-blood bravely won their wreaths of mar-
    tial glory.
One fate unites them evermore ; one column bears each name—
Forgotten now are feuds of yore — one people guards their
    fame.

THE CANADIAN FARMER'S SONG.

LET the cities proud boast long and loud
    Of their palaces fair and grand ;
In the country wide, spread on every side,
    Are the works of our Father's hand.
Though our fate may seem, to some idler's dream,
    A toilsome and weary lot.
Yet peace and health are the priceless wealth
    That are found in the settler's cot.
We are freemen good—not a slave ever stood
    On our loved Canadian soil—
No tyrant's power can withhold for an hour
    The fruits of our honest toil.

Though to Britain is due love loyal and true—
    Where the bones of our fathers rest—
Yet the forest-land, with its rivers grand,
    Is the land that we love the best.
Here our sons in pride grow side by side,
    The joy of our peaceful hours ;
And our daughters fair as the wild-flowers rare
    That bloom in the forest bowers.

Tho' the son of the soil has a life of toil,
    Yet calm and sweet is his rest ;

He wakes from his dreams, ere the Day-King's beams
    Have shone on the blue-jay's nest.
He drinks of the rills that gush from the hills,
    And the soil he tills is his own;
And as happy and free as a king is he—
    Who bows but to God alone.

When the welcome Spring comes on golden wing,
    In the sugar-bush, blithe and free,
We gather with care the life-blood rare,
    That flows from the maple tree.
And we plough and sow in hope, for we know,
    If we waste the beautiful Spring,
Our regret will be vain, when in Winter's reign
    Gaunt Famine is on the wing.

When the Autumn yields the fruits of the fields,
    A reward for our toil is given;
We thankfully take her gifts, which bespeak
    The love of our Father in heaven.
When the wintry blast goes howling past,
    Spreading sorrow and want on its way,
By the bright maple fire, safe from rude Winter's ire,
    We sit at the close of the day.
And our songs of praise we joyfully raise,
    High over stern Nature's strife,
As to Heaven ascend thanks for home and friends,
    And the joys of a Farmer's life.

A CENTENARY SONG.

[The *Quebec Gazette* is the oldest newspaper in Canada. On completing its 100th year, a centenary number was issued, for which these lines were written.]

LIKE the harbinger star that glimmers afar,
   · And heralds the rosy morn,
A spirit of light, in the darksome night
   Of the bygone years I was born.
   The first of my race in this happy place,
     Where Freedom and Peace abide,
For a hundred years, amid hopes and fears,
   I have breasted both wind and tide.

This land so fair, which may now compare
   With the brightest beneath the sun,
Was a wilderness wild, where the forest-child
   Roamed in pride, when my race begun.
But the light has broke—'neath the woodman's stroke
   The forests have melted away ;
The golden grain waves o'er hill and plain,
   Where the wolf and the bear then lay ;
Where the wigwam rude of the Indian stood,
   Beneath the sheltering pines,
The stately spire, like a beacon fire,
   In the sunset radiance shines.

Like the zephyr that blows o'er the frozen snows,
  And tells of the coming spring,
Ere the winter had fled, I silently sped,
  On eager and buoyant wing,
To each peaceful spot, where the emigrant's cot
  Was built in the forest grand :
Like a messenger-bird, I brought him word
  From his loved and native land.

I have toiled to illume the mental gloom,
  Which clouded the virgin soil;
The tidings I brought and the truths I taught
  Have lightened the woes of toil :
I have echoed around whatever was found
  By the seekers in mines of truth,
And tirelessly sought, with the light of thought,
  To quicken the mind of youth.

Thro' Times rapid flight, I saw with delight
  The growth of our national tree ;
Till it spreads with pride its branches wide,
  And shelters the brave and free.
The progress of truth, with the joy of youth,
  I have watched since the day of my birth ;
As like dawning light, which expels the night,
  It scattered the mists of earth.

Thro' the silent tread of the years that have fled,
  I have witnessed the birth and decay

Of many a peer, whose transient career
  Shone with brilliant and meteor-like ray :
I have seen the fair—and the fortunate heir
  Of royalty, riches, and fame,—
The noblest of birth, the greatest on earth,
  Pass away like the lowliest name.

I have chronicled things, both of peasants and kings,
  The fortunes of rich and of poor ;
For beauty and power may die in an hour—
  There are sorrows for all to endure.
I have gathered with care, the melodies rare,
  That from poet and minstrel have flown ;
And have soothed and blessed many a weary breast,
  With their tender and mystical tone.

I have told of the birth that brought joy to the hearth—
  Of the bliss of the nuptial day,—
Of the icy breath of relentless death,
  Laying hopeful hearts in the clay.
I carried the fame of Britain's name
  To the hearts of her children true,
When over the deep, came with thrilling sweep,
  The echoes of Waterloo.

The friends, once my pride, have faded and died—
  The hearts that I gladdened are still ;
Yet I glide on my way, without pause or delay,
  Like a murmuring forest rill,

Well knowing that those, whether friends or foes,
　Who may hear my centennial song,
Like those whom I weep, shall soon sink to sleep
　With the silent, undreaming throng.

Though a hundred years, with their hopes and fears,
　Have vanished with surging roar,
The furrows of age do not wrinkle a page,
　And my eye is as keen as of yore :
Then, one hearty cheer for my hundredth year!
　Truth, Freedom, and Peace are my toast !
If my friends prove true, as all friends should do,
　I shall never desert my post.

Though over my head a century's fled,
　With its wearisome toil and strife,
I feel strongly inclined, if the world be kind,
　To take a new lease of my life.
In the coming years shall be joys and tears,
　And changes, like those of the past;
And work to be done, and fields to be won,
　As long as the world shall last.

Miscellaneous Pieces.

DEATH OF DR. THOMAS COKE.

They that be wise shall shine as the brightness of the firmament; and they that turn many to righteousness, as the stars for ever and ever. —Dan. xii : 3.

TOSSED on the billows, far from the shore,
    A vessel was onward sweeping ;
Which a band of Christian heroes bore,
    Thro' winds and waves in her keeping.

They are sailing on to a clime unknown,
    Leaving home and friends far behind them ;
To tribes where the truth has never shone,
    And fetters of darkness bind them.

But one of brave and saintly life,
    Whose locks are thin and hoary,
'Mid the wailing din of the ocean's strife
    Is nearing the haven of glory.

He often had cross'd the western main,
    On love's unselfish mission ;
But the land of his birth shall never again
    Rise to gladden his failing vision.

No signal, sound, or sight gave token
    That death was hovering near ;
Not a farewell word, in kindness spoken,
    Was whispered in friendship's ear.

'Twas night on the deep, and he sank to rest,
    Wrapt in dreams of hope and duty ;
But, ere morn had broke o'er the ocean's breast,
    He had flown to the land of beauty.

None watched life's low and ebbing tide,
    No words of mortals cheer him ;
Like the prophet of Sinai, alone he died
    With none but Jehovah near him.

Slowly they lower'd, with mournful mien,
    To the deeps where the storms were sleeping,
That hero-father, o'er whom was seen
    Two nations sadly weeping.

Tho' he never beheld that pagan shore,
    Whose darkness stir'd his pity,
And pass'd by a nearer way before,
    To the pure and pearly city ;

Yet his spirit lived in the hearts sublime,
    That his loss o'ercast with sadness ;
And they carried to India's burning clime
    The gospel of peace and gladness.

Where the light of day is never shed,
  Far beneath the rolling surges,
He sleeps in his pearl-lit ocean bed,
  And the waves above sing his dirges.

The vessels that glide o'er his pulseless breast
  May cast their shadows above him ;
Like the prophet, too, his place of rest
  Is unknown to all who love him.

Tho' still the sleep of his dreamless head,
  His name kindles brave endeavor :
He shall rise, when the sea shall yield her dead,
  And shine as a star forever.

A WELCOME

TO REV. W. MORLEY PUNSHON, M.A.

HERALD of the hallowed cross,
    Teaching truth in words of fire,
  Builder of the "lofty rhyme,"
    Master of the tuneful lyre,
  Welcome o'er the billowy deep ;
    Canada with joy doth greet thee ;
  Tho' behind thee friends may weep,
    Here with loving hearts we meet thee.

14

Ere we saw thy face, there came,
  Floating o'er the silver sea,
Echoes of thy words of flame,
  CHIMES of sacred melody,
Rich with rare delight for all.
  Still may truths thy lips declare
Thousands bring from Satan's thrall,
  Liberty and life to share.

Welcome! from the dear old land,
  Where our fathers' ashes rest,
Whose heroic deeds inspire
  Grateful pride in every breast.
Albion's gifted son, to thee
  Give we love and honor due—
To this land, where all are free,
  Welcome! we are BRITONS too.

To the land of lake and river,
  Yielding labor rich increase,—
Crush'd by lordly tyrant never,
  Where we worship God in peace,
Each Canadian gives a welcome,
  Free from faithless flattery's arts—
Welcome to our wide Dominion!
  Welcome to our homes and hearts!

ROBERT BURNS.

WHILE thousands loud thy glory sing,
A wreath of forest flowers I bring,
   As thy birth-day returns ;
With sad and warm regard allied,
I sing of him, his country's pride,
   Immortal ROBERT BURNS !

Old Scotia's sons their plaudits give—
Nor there alone his name shall live,
   And his fair fame be sung ;
Wherever Britain's flag's unfurl'd,
From clime to clime, around the world,
   Thy starry name hath rung.

His was a warm and kindly heart,
That did for human suffering smart
   With deep and gen'rous love.
Such knowledge of the human breast,
As few of mortal race possest,
   Was given him from above.

No crouching slave to wealth was he ;
In numbers fearless, warm, and free,
   The poor man's claims he sang ;
In praise of manhood, truth, and love,

And all that gen'rous hearts approve,
  His thrilling lyrics rang.

No common gifts could so delight;
Rare tenderness and fire unite
  Their powers at his control:
Touch'd by his skilful, master hand,
The lyre gave forth, strains sweet and grand,
  To melt and thrill the soul.

But gifts of genius, wealth, or power,
To mortals given are golden dower,
  Bestowed by God the Just;
And he that Heaven's own charge betrays,
And turns his feet from Wisdom's ways,
  Must answer for his trust.

Hence Burns, the wreath I twine for thee
Is not from shades of cyprus free,
  Nor tints of dark regret;
That gifts so lofty and divine
Should minister at Bacchus' shrine,
  Awakens sorrow yet.

When Passion's stormy billows roll'd,
No living, steadfast faith control'd,
  To guide thee on toward heaven;
But like a vessel helmless left,
Of power to breast the storm bereft,
  So wert thou wildly driven.

The friends of purity and truth,
Who mark the promise of thy youth,
   And then its sad decline,
While drunkards madly shout thy name,
And fill their goblets to thy fame,
   Must weep o'er lives like thine.

I would not break the still repose,
Nor with unkindness speak of those,
   Who sleep beneath the sod:
I would not spread again to view
The errors of a mortal, who
   Has gone to meet his God;

But, if from his misguided lyre
Flow strains that fan unholy fire,
   And conscience hush to sleep;—
And if a blessed angel mourns,
To look upon the life of Burns,
   Should Truth weak silence keep?

And when his blighted life is praised,
It gilds the vices which debased
   And stained his eagle mind;
And falsely hides the danger near
Those thoughtless souls, who downward steer,
   While syren pleasures bind.

Do gifts of genius Heaven bestows,
To bless and brighten Earth's dark woes,

O'er wounds of sorrow's poisoned dart
  Love's pitying eyes were bent;
She wept o'er sufferings of the heart,
  She could no more prevent.

She wept, till wearied grief grew calm,
  Then sighed that grief was vain;
But saw with joy, her tears, like balm,
  Had soothed the sufferer's pain.

Then Love arose on buoyant wing,
  To her the work was given,
To broken, bleeding hearts to bring
  The healing balm of heaven.

Ere since, where Sorrow's blight is shed,
  Or wounded hearts appear,
Has gentle Love in pity fled,
  And healed them with a tear.

AN ELEGY:

ON THE DEATH OF REV. JAMES SPENCER, M.A.

A S one who sadly watches, from the shore,
A vessel sinking in a stormy sea,
Whose fate a thousand hearts in vain deplore—
SPENCER, I feel for thee !

And can it be, that thou art also passed
Across the dark and melancholy tide ;
Struck down, unwarned, by death's relentless blast,
In manhood's strength and pride ?

And shall we see thy manly form no more,
Nor with warm friendship clasp thine honest hand,
Until we meet, with life's fierce struggles o'er,
In the bright spirit land ?

Lay him to rest—while summer leaves are dying,
And fading glory tints the vernal bowers,
While autumn winds their mournful dirge are sighing—
Among the faded flowers.

Not with a hoary head, at set of sun—
Not with prophetic voice of slow decay—
Long ere his work of faith and love seemed done,
In the lone grave he lay.

At tidings of thy swift and sad decline,
From many a heart warm tears of grief shall flow;
Though thou art now where deathless glories shine,
    We mourn thy loss below.

Though grief cannot our vanished hopes restore,
Let faithful friends with tears embalm his name :
To live enshrined in honest hearts, is more
    Than wreaths of earthly fame.

Nor yet with wasting sorrow vainly weep,
When at his post a standard-bearer falls ;
But each the lessons in remembrance keep,
    Which this sad hour recalls.

Within his breast a manly soul he bore,
That never quailed, when truth and duty led,
Upon his path, when darkness gathered o'er,
    Celestial light was shed.

Freedom and truth he loved with fearless love—
Falsehood and guile he scorned with honest hate—
Unbribed by flattery, and by threats unmoved,
    Heaven nerved for every fate.

He was no man of smooth and silvery tongue,
No crouching sycophant to power or pride ;
Fearless and stern his honest accents rung,
    When justice was denied.

Thus all the hero hearts of mortal birth,
Like him have bowed to death's mysterious sway;
All the great souls, whose footsteps hallowed earth,
   Were hastening to decay.

All here is transient. Earth is wet with tears.
The friends we love—the bliss for which we sigh—
The love that gladdens, and the hope that cheers,
   Like flowers of summer die.

There is a brighter world, beyond the strife,
Where blinding mists dissolve in limpid air:
All the perplexing ills that darken life
   Shall be unravelled there.

Spencer, farewell! would that my broken lays
Had power to keep thy honored memory bright;
But thou art crowned with amaranthine bays,
   In the pure world of light.

Whate'er thy faults, I dare not scan them now—
Thou art with God—let erring man forbear—
And he, who weaves this garland for thy brow,
   May soon himself be there.

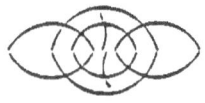

THE INVISIBLE LAND.

THERE is a vast and shadowy clime—
A region deep-hid in the bosom of Time—
Where Hope is throned as a sceptred queen,
And Fancy's fairest visions are seen.
A land by created foot never trod,
Whose treasures are seen by none but God.
For a thick-woven veil hangs for evermore
Between mortal eyes and that beautiful shore.
Thence out of the darkness joyously rings
Anthems, which Hope to Fancy sings,
Kindling such joy in the listening heart,
As only the carols of Hope can impart;
Or sorrowful plaints of Fear and Dismay,
Which darken the light of the brightest day.

Not a child of Earth, whatever his lot,
To reign in a palace, or weep in a cot,
But feel that for him that region contains
Either fountains of joy, or verdureless plains.
And ever, as Time, with his noiseless hand
Rolls back the veil from this cloud-covered land,
And sheds the light of the swift-footed years,
On the scenes of their flickering hopes and fears,
They watch with deep and passionate gaze,
To learn what is stored in the coming days;

It may be a gift, most precious and rare,
Or a burden of blighting sorrow and care;
For thorns of sorrow and joy-flowers bloom
Thickly, side by side, in that region of gloom.

It has isles of beauty in glassy seas,
Whose air is balmy and skies are fair;
And springs and summers, whose every breeze
Is laden with fragrance and music rare;
And regions so desolate, barren, and cold,
Their starless wretchedness cannot be told.
It has hours, like angels with golden wings,
Which glide through the light their radiance flings;
And hours, like angels of darkness and death,
Congealing the blood with their icy breath;
Bringing cups of bitterest anguish and pain,
Which the children of sorrow and toil must drain.

And there lives not a victim of Pride and Power,
But hopes in the Future to win release;
But dreams of some bright and golden hour,
When the reign of Oppression and Wrong shall cease;
And Truth and Love, with their beauty and might,
Shall banish the sombre-hued shadows of night.
Not a toiler who plods 'neath a burden of care,
But dreams of relief and liberty there;
Not a weary seeker for truth and light,
But waits for a morning, tranquil and bright,
When the shadows of Doubt and Darkness shall fly,
And visions of beauty shall gladden his eye.

O who could endure the burdens of life !
The heart-aches of Falsehood, of Envy, and strife ;
The gloom-laden years of misfortune and grief,—
The baffled schemes that are void of relief,
Who heard not the joy-notes of Hope, as she sings
Of the benisons, Time, on his pathway flings?
There is bread for the hungry, and wealth for the poor,
And fountains of pleasure whose waters are pure ;
Rest for the weary, and sight for the blind,
And freedom from all that o'ershadows the mind.
There is solace for Sorrow's woe-laden plaint,
Truth for the seeker, and strength for the faint.

These voices which float from the cloud-covered shore,
Whispers prophetic of what lies before,
Though they kindle baseless and fanciful dreams,
Attemper our fate with their golden gleams.
Like the broken plank, that has often bore,
The ship-wrecked wretch to the rocky shore,
Though frail as the airy phantoms of Night,
With a glance dispelled by the morning light,
Yet they oft, to the struggling and fainting heart,
New vigor, new hope, and life impart ;
And nerve with the thought of a time to come,
When the voices of Envy and Fear shall be dumb;
And Truth, and Justice, and Love shall reign,
Shedding peaceful light o'er life's misty main.

DEACON GRIMES.

A Man of character and mark,
  Well known in church and street,—
A wiser, or a graver face
  You very seldom meet;—
A sturdy pillar of the church;
  Punctual as Sabbath chimes,
With stern decorum in his place,
  Is honest Deacon Grimes.

In doctrine truly orthodox,
  In dealings sternly just;
And, though his talents are but small,
  He does not let them rust.
That he has virtues all must own,
  And good his zeal has wrought;
But he has some unpleasant ways,
  That make it dearly bought.

He has a certain type of creed,
  Religion, mien, and grace;
And all who do not bear his marks,
  He deems in doubtful case.
'Tis odd, he never seems to think
  That such a thing might be,
That some one else should know the truth,
  And love it well as he.

He magnifies a little thing,
  Some crotchet of his own,
As if the life of Church and State
  All hung on that alone.
He's down upon all modern ways,
  Thinks them a sorry sight,
But thinks that things, when he was young,
  Were somewhere nearly right.

He's very keen to mark a fault,
  Of mercy little knows,—
On every weakness—but his own—
  He deals unsparing blows.
The wrong are those who dare condemn
  His favorite plans and views:
And to be right, approve his schemes,
  And other schemes abuse.

In all the playful sports of youth,
  He gravest wrong descries;
And strangely thinks the young should see
  All nature through his eyes.
That merry hearts, which gaily bound
  To hope's entrancing chimes,
Should feel and act, in everything,
  Like sober Deacon Grimes.

He thinks it shows his pious zeal,
  For all his views to fight;

Though it may rouse opposing minds,
  With other views of right.
And yet, there's none can well dispute,
  Regard, in every case,
For what his brethren think would be
  A better sign of grace.

Though zealous for the church's weal,
  If you reject *his* plan,
You need not look for help from him,
  For he'll do all he can
To show that such a course has been
  A great mistake for you,—
To vindicate himself, and make
  His prophecies come true.

I question not his zeal, nor doubt
  That he is quite sincere,—
He may have sweeter thoughts within,
  Than outwardly appear ;
And still, I think, he never yet
  Has fairly understood,
That selfish zeal bereft of love,
  May do more harm than good.

And, though he may be sound at core,
  There's many a sinner round,
With whom more kind and pleasant ways,
  And charity are found.
15

If piety must make me like
  The subject of these rhymes,
I'd rather have some other kind,
  Than be like Deacon Grimes.

LEAD THOU ME ON.

LEAD Thou me on. My path is steep:
  Beset with foes I cannot see—
Father thy child in safety keep,
  My strength is all from Thee.

When clouds and darkness round me close,
And fierce temptations sorely press,
Hold Thou my hand; repel my foes;
  With calm endurance bless.

Forgive my weak, distrustful fears;
Let thankful love my portion be,
Till, safe from conflicts, doubts, and tears,
  I rest above with Thee.

LOVE.

E sage explorers of thoughts shadowy deeps,
    Say, what is Love, if by your lore ye know ?
For Love the bard his rarest garland keeps—
Of Love, by turns, the maiden sings and weeps—
    From Love's unfathomed fountains strangely flow
    Joy's sunniest streams, and Sorrow's darkest tide;
As if alike to heaven and hell allied.

Love is the offspring of a purer clime,
    Not native to a blighted world like this;
The lone memorial of a happier time,
    Ere faithless falsehood coiled within a kiss,—
    Or sin had marred and poisoned human bliss.
It blooms on earth a bright perennial flower—
Its nature hid, we only know its power.

Love nerves the arm for action most sublime,
    And bindeth heart to heart in holiest ties;
Where'er she breathes o'er earth's ungenial clime,
    Fair flowers of joy on barren heaths arise,
    And kindly stars from dull and cloudy skies
Shed golden gleams o'er many a suffering lot;
For where she smiles oppression is forgot.

She gives us tears to weep for mortal woe,
　And faith and fortitude her glance inspires ;
She kindles joy to rapture's warmest glow,
　And lingers oft when baffled Hope retires :—
　She gently quenches Envy's rising fires,—
Round human weakness Pity's mantle flings,
And takes from Poverty her sharpest stings.

In childhood's years, a mother's tireless eye
　Watched o'er our helplessness, with loving care,—
Did all our wants with tenderness supply—
　Did all our petulance with patience bear,
　And all our joys and sorrows kindly share.
Through every stage the genial power we feel,—
A star to brighten, and a balm to heal.

In life's gay spring, when the attractive grace,
　And sunny smile of some fair youthful form
Thrill'd with a joy that time cannot efface,
　Love's sacred flame burn'd high and warm,
　And scatter'd rainbows o'er each gathering storm—
Then every object flash'd in golden light,
And every hour was freighted with delight.

Then Hope her radiant pinions lightly spread,
　And coming years their promised joys unfold,
With visions bright the inner bliss was fed;
　A cloudless sunshine richest lustre shed,
　And turn'd the rocky path of life to gold—

Graved on the soul a truth unknown before,
That joy is deepened as we love the more.

In manhood, 'mid the surging cares of life,
  How sweet the solace and how sure the aid,
Of Heaven's best gift, a kind and faithful wife;
  Tho' friends may change, and poverty invade,
  When fairest flowers in dust and darkness fade.—
And envious slander blasts a guiltless name,
Her love and truth but burn with brighter flame.

When wasting age bedims the searching eye,
  And gently frosts the raven locks of youth;
When vigorous forms in helpless suffering lie,
  Ready to gather up the feet and die,
  Sweeter than life is filial love and truth,
Watching with grief the failing pulse and breath,—
Lighting with tenderness the vale of death.

Though sin perverts, and turns to springs of pain,
  The purest rills that in life's valleys shine,—
Tho' purest snow-flakes earthy dross may stain,
  And rarest flowers some poisonous juice contain,
  They are not less of origin divine:
And every pulse of pure and truthful love
Makes mortal spirits more like God above.

'Tis heaven's unchanging law, that all must grow
  To share the nature of the things they love;

If clings the heart to what is base and low,
   Its power to darken and degrade we prove
In guilty stains, that time cannot remove.
Unhallowed love forges a chain, to bind
In sordid serfdom man's immortal mind.

But if we love the noble and divine,
   Shall potent Love, with silent, subtle art,
Their beauty with the inner life entwine,
   And stamp their image on the loving heart;
   For as the oak exalts the clinging vine,
The loving tendrils of the heart forgiven
Take hold of God, and lift us nearer heaven.

O! what were earth, with all its wide domains,
   Its lordly mountains and its boundless seas;
Its waving forests and its fertile plains;
   Its homes of splendor, luxury, and ease—
   Its scenes of beauty, formed to bless and please,
With golden worlds o'er-canopied above?
Joyless were all without the light of love:

A barren desert, where no living stream
   Pours life and gladness all along its way;—
A gloomy solitude, where never beam
   Those rays divine that turn life's night to day,
   Through which no friendly, ruthful angels stray;
A mountain bleak, where freezing tempests sweep,
And hungry wolves unpitying vigils keep.

If Love's bright beams on earth no longer shone,
  And tyrant Passion owned not her control,—
If envy, pride, and avarice alone·
  Gave law and purpose to the servile soul,
  Steering it onward to sin's fatal goal,
The dark eclipse not seraph tongue could tell—
A loveless world would be a rayless hell.

In yon bright sphere, where sinless spirits sing,
  Love is the fruitful, heaven-entrancing theme—
Of joys immortal the exhaustless spring—
  Here shines the Godhead's most effulgent beam;
  For Love evolved the vast and mystic scheme,
Thro' which a guilty world may be forgiven;
And Love alone can ripen us for heaven.

OLD LETTERS.

USING alone at the midnight hour,
    Lull'd by the night-wind's sweep,
I am chained by the thrilling and mystic power,
    Which these time-worn relics keep.

Old yellow leaves, ye speak of the hours
    Ere the blossoms of life were blighted;
When Hope sang in green and fragrant bowers
    The lays which my youth delighted.

Ye come like waifs o'er the ocean tide,
    From a clime that is now far away,
Where Spring ever lingers in virgin pride,
    And beauty outlives decay.

Old letters from youthful friends of yore,
    Wide-scattered, and long forgot:
Some have won renown—many more
    Never gained the port they sought.

There are surges of feeling pensive and deep,
    As faces and forms forgotten start
To life from their silent death-like sleep,
    In the grave of a living heart.

I retrace my pathway of sunlight and tears
　To the spring-time, when life was new,
Ere the scorching heat of the weary years
　Had drunk up its pearly dew.

Here, too, are others, that bear a name,
　Once could kindle a tell-tale glow—
They were cherished records, with words of flame,
　In the joy-tinted long-ago.

As I read in the silence, the past is unroll'd—
　I live over those days gone by,
When Hope wove her tissues of dazzling gold,
　And life had a starry sky.

I remember the rapture that flooded my soul,
　The palaces built on the sand,
As I read, like a message from heaven, each scroll
　That was traced by her angel hand.

Then the world was bathed in beauty and love,
　The future rose cloudless and bright;
For the earth beneath and the stars above
　Re-echoed the heart's delight.

Alas! that in life, like the ocean deeps,
　None may trust in the tranquil hour;
In the treach'rous pause, while the tempest sleeps,
　It is girded with fiercer power.

But swiftly my vision of light disappears—
    Dark shadows come over the scene—
There is sorrow and joy in my gushing tears,
    As I think of what might have been.

How vainly I weep o'er incurable woes!
    My life-star, so cherished and dear,
'Neath the summer's green and the winter's snows,
    Has been sleeping for many a year.

I am left like the stem of a faded flower,
    Whose beautiful petals are dust;
My life is all winter since that dark hour,
    But I murmur not—Heaven is just.

Frail fragments, thrown from the wrecks of life
    On a sunless and desolate shore,
Ye have strangely flashed, o'er the heart's hidden strife,
    A gleam of the sunlight of yore.

THE DYING BARD.

HE was bowed beneath sorrow and age, as he sang
    The last lay of his weary life ;
He stood on the verge of the spirit-land,
Like a ship with sails by the zephyrs fanned,
Ready to launch from his natal strand,
    To return no more to its strife.

"O bear me forth 'neath the open sky,
    While the Earth wears her robes of green,
For I fain would gaze on the beautiful world,
When the banners of eve are gaily unfurled,
And the glassy streams, by the zephyr curled,
    Brighten the tranquil scene.

The current of waning life is low—
    I shall soon win release from pain—
But the forests and fields, the lakes and streams,
The beautiful tints in which Nature gleams,
Have given such joy to my youthful dreams,
    That I long to behold them again.

I have found every hour of my care-haunted life
    A response to my joy and my woe,

In the emerald hills and the waving trees,
In the beautiful flowers that scented the breeze,
In the songs of the birds and the hum of the bees,
    Let me bid them farewell ere I go.

Let me rest awhile 'neath this branching elm,
    A spot that was sacred of yore,
And gaze on the mountain's golden crest,—
The crimson glow that suffuses the west,
On the gorgeous Eve which I love the best—
    I shall never behold them more.

This hour recalls my life's opening morn,
    When the love of beauty was strong,
When I wandered a careless happy boy
Through the forest wilds, with a speechless joy;
Communing with Nature was sweeter employ,
    Than to blend with the soulless throng.

Then I listened with joy to the wonderful strains
    Of Poesie's deathless seers:
They bore me up as with eagle flight,—
They opened new worlds of beauty and light,
And thrilled my soul with a magical might,
    Till my gladness dissolved in tears.

The draughts I drank from Nature and song
    Waked longings I could not control—
I too would sing of Truth and of Man,—

Of the heroes who battled in Freedom's van,—
Of all noble deeds since the world began,—
　　Of the heights and deeps of the soul ;

And of all the grand and glorious things,
　　Which the caskets of beauty keep.
Then visions of fame unrolled to my sight,
I said, I will sing of the true and the right,
Oppression and Wrong I will fearlessly smite,
　　Till the world awake from its sleep.

Great thoughts flashed over my burning brain,
　　With the joy of a new-found world ;
With peerless lustre and beauty fraught,
So grand, that I vainly and toilfully sought
For language to clothe each wonderful thought—
　　They died in my heart impearled.

My dreams have vanished, like mists of air,
　　The hopes, once most precious, are dead ;
The toils of my life seem fruitless and vain ;
No monuments tell of my mental pain ;
No harvest waves with the golden grain,
　　That sprang from the seeds which I spread.

The diamond thoughts I dug from the mine—
　　The lays of beauty I tunefully sang—
The tales of sorrow and faith sincere,
That spoke to the heart of peasant and peer,

Which I fancied the world must pause to hear,
    Unheeded in darkness rang.

The flowers I brought from the forest shades—
    The pearls of thought from the deep—
All fell on the sordid, gold-seeking throng,
As a wild-bird's tender and passionate song,
On the ocean shore, when the winds are strong,
    And the billows wrathfully sweep.

When I pencilled the future with promise bright,
    And hurled at Folly my keenest dart;
When I wove my thoughts in a beautiful wreath,
And sang of the mystical power of faith,
Which raises the soul above all beneath,
    They sneered at the songs of my heart.

Like a silent stream in Canadian woods,
    Concealed from the light of the sun,
That softly glides on its lonely way,
In Winter's snow, and in Summer's ray,
The world and its strife unheard, far away,
    So my sorrowful race was run.

The sun of my life is low in the west—
    The shades of the twilight descend—
Yet, why should I sorrow with fruitless tears,
O'er the failure that darkens the vanished years?

How worthless the glory of earth appears,
   When nearing our journey's end !

Yet truths I have scattered in trembling hope,
  Like grain that sleeps in the frozen soil,
Awaiting the genial vernal showers,
When I rest in the grave, may give fruits and flowers,
Whose fragrance shall gladden the desolate hours
   Of some child of sorrow and toil.

The wise and the good have bravely taught
   That no earnest effort is vain ;—
A higher success than the plaudits of fame,
A richer gift than a laurel'd name,
Is a life that is true to a lofty aim,
   And free from a guilty stain.

As the glory of earth recedes and expires,
  Faith opens a world of joy to my sight,—
I hail the dawn of a brighter day—
The shadows of night are floating away—
O who amid darkness and death would stay,
   From that kingdom of glory and light?

There is balm for the earth-worn, weary heart;—
  There tears of sorrow shall never flow ;—
There the Poet's harp shall be sweetly strung
To loftier hymns, than on earth was sung,

And heaven may listen to strains that rung,
  Unheeded and scorned below.

Farewell ye mountains, ye rivers and lakes,
  That won my deep and passionate love :
Ye never could fill my longing breast,—
Ye never could calm my heart's unrest,—
Ye are only types and shadows, at best,
  Of the beauty and grandeur above."

While he sang his last lay, the golden-eyed sun
  Softly sank in the clouds of the west—
The sentinel hills stood silent and lone—
The birds sang their vespers with tenderest tone—
The zephyrs of Eve breathed a sorrowful moan,
  As his spirit passed home to its rest.

WINTER MUSINGS.*

FROM the bleak ice-fields of the polar zone,
    The dreary empire of perpetual snows,
Where Desolation rears her tyrant throne
    And icy palaces, secure from foes,
Heralds of winter, frosty breezes moan,
    Breaking autumnal stillness and repose :
Nature in calm suspense, sombre and dumb,
Awaits the change she feels must shortly come.

The light grows dim ; the breeze is soft and low ;
    The sky is muffled with a leaden cloud :
The air is filled with glist'ning flakes of snow,
    Fair, fragile forms, which noiselessly enshroud
The rugged earth, in robes of dazzling light,
And kindly screen her nakedness from sight.

Bewildering beauty, purity, and grace,
    Fall like a vision glorious and serene,
Of some pure world where sin has left no trace,
    More blest and fair than mortal eye hath seen ;
Kindling within my heart a fervent sigh
    For holier bliss than earth's low gifts supply,—

---

*This is a portion of a poem, entitled *The Canadian Year*, the whole of which could not conveniently be included in this volume.

For that far land where souls refined, forgiven,
Are pure and stainless as the stars of heaven.

Each tree displays a graceful, snowy crest,
    There's light and glory spread on every side ;
Nature, in spotless ermine, gaily drest,
    Sits cold and beautiful, king Winter's bride :
Rivers and lakes, congealed by his chill breath,
Are mute and waveless in the grasp of Death.

The drifting snows that whirl in every breeze—
    The noisy skaters on the frozen stream—
The creaking plaint of swaying forest trees—
    The merry bells of every passing team—
The lengthening shadow and the sinking sun—
All loudly signal Winter's reign begun.

The silver falls, that all the summer night
    Sung its hoarse dirges to the listening air,
Is voiceless now.   In melancholy plight
    The stately trees stand, bannerless and bare,
As if their beauty and their pride were o'er,
And Nature's pulse would throb with life no more.

Still looming o'er the boundless waste of snow,
    The balsam, spruce, and sturdy hemlock rise ;
Like faithful friends, whose hearts no coldness know
    When life's bleak winter darkens summer skies.
While dreary barrenness o'erspreads the scene,
They stand enrobed in amaranthine green.

The beech-leaves rustling in the frosty blast,
 While 'neath the snows their frail companions lie,
Portray the hardy children of the past,
 Whose lengthened years see, with regretful eye,
All early friendships buried in the tomb,
And linger but to witness lonelier gloom.

Where are the birds, whose softly warbled strains,
 Sweet as the music heavenly lute imparts,
Serenely floated over hills and plains,
 In notes of joy, for worn and weary hearts?
At morn—at eve, we miss their hymns of praise,
And silent Nature listens for their lays.

The hardy wood-pecker disdains to flee;
 His hopeful voice rings through the silent wood:
Gliding with jerking flight, from tree to tree,
 By ceaseless tapping gains his daily food—
Emblem of patient industry and toil.
No storm can baffle and no danger foil.

We miss the silver gleams of stream and lake,
 Which mirrored back the glories of the sky—
The grateful green of forest, field, and brake,—
 The gentle flowers which teach us, while they die,
Lessons of patient hope and lowly trust
In Him, who drew their beauty from the dust.

The western skies with fiery gold aglow—
 A belt of flame resting on mountains bare—

Chill blistering breezes, hissing as they go
  All sorrow-laden through the desert air,
With fierce delight to drift the powdery snow—
  The creaking sleighs and cloudy breath declare,
With voice prophetic at the sunset hour,
The coming night shall feel the frost-king's power.

Sad is his fate, with chilling cold oppress'd,
  Who on such night mistakes his homeward way;
And sinks, o'ercome, on snowy couch to rest,
  Till life in dreamy torpor ebbs away;
While anxious friends his lengthened absence mourn,
And watch for him who never shall return.

When the harsh days in twilight shades expire—
  'Tis well the sternest days are soonest gone—
In forest homes, around the maple fire,
  The household gather when their toil is done ;
While howling storms disturb the midnight air,
Content and peace securely nestle there.

Communing of the sunny days of youth,
  Of friends and times which Memory sacred keeps,
With her who lights with love's unwaning truth
  His lowly lot, and lulls his fears to sleep;
Or else in silence listening to the storms,
  Grateful for sheltering home and simple store,
Some useful implement the father forms—
  A birchen broom to sweep the cottage floor,

Or handle for the axe, whose strokes o'erthrow
The ancient woods, and lay their monarchs low.

The thrifty mother, as she spins or knits,
    Watches the children's gambols on the floor—
The silent youth who in the corner sits,
    Whose eager eyes with rapt delight explore
Some borrowed volume, now, by fancy led,
Fights in the battles of the warlike dead.

Ah! many a lowly home unknown contains
    A heart that Heaven has touched with sacred fire;
Stern is the conflict patient hope maintains,
    When all the powers of adverse fate conspire,
And Fortune from the thirsty seeker's eyes
Withholds the founts for which he vainly sighs.

Yet snow-clad Canada—Heaven-favored land—
    I love thee best. Thy name, alone, awakes
Visions of forests green and mountains grand—
    Of regal rivers and of ocean lakes,
Where freedom's banners proudly wave;
Home of the free, and refuge of the slave.

Let France or Italy, or proud and abject Spain
    Boast of their balmy air and brilliant skies;
And many an ancient and stupendous fane,
    Which fills the traveller with untold surprise,
Dark bigotry and tyrant power combined,
There strangle freedom and enslave the mind.

I envy not the fairest lands, whose youth
   Freedom and Truth only in dreams can bless.
Here no proud despot's word can stifle truth—
   No lordly tyrants honest toil oppress.
Land, where to.live is to be proudly free,
May no dark fate ere sever me from thee.

Now while the lazy bear for months retires,
   And like an anchorite in sullen mood,
While Winter reigns, nor friend nor food requires,
   Far up the creeks of the primeval wood,
While snowy vestments shroud the frozen soil,
The hardy lumbermen pursue their toil.

All day, their busy axes ceaseless ring,
   Felling the pine and elm for Albion's mart ;
At night around the shanty fire they sing
   Some tuneful melodies, devoid of art ;
Or else, with merry pranks beguile the hour,
Till dreamy Sleep asserts her gentle power.

When Spring unlocks the streams, and melts the snows,
   They leave their rude and solitary sphere.
When fierce and strong the angry current flows,
   Fearless their cumbrous rafts, with skill, they steer
Down the broad Ottawa, or rapid Trent,
While merry songs proclaim their calm content.

In the recesses of the pathless woods,
   The Indian hunter tracks, with noiseless feet,

The timid deer,—thro' drifts, o'er frozen floods
   And tangled swamps,—silent and fleet,
Hungry and worn, he roams from place to place,
Till night or fortune ends his weary chase.

Meanwhile, the partner of his rugged lot
   Sits, lone and patient, in her fragile tent :
Quaint fancies with the birchen bark are wrought—
   In toiling loneliness her life is spent.
Earth's glitt'ring prizes, donors of unrest,
Kindle no wish in her untutored breast.

When Night has spread her ebon mantle round
   The wintry world, phantoms of anxious doubt
Come trooping thro' the darkness, till the sound
   Of his approaching steps puts Fear to rout ;
As robbers flee when friendly aid draws nigh,
Her gloomy thoughts before his presence fly.

His new-slain deer supplies a rich repast—
   They breath no wish for more luxurious fare—
Upon their hemlock couch they sink to rest,
   Unjarred by envy, undisturbed by care.
The darkest lot becomes serenely bright,
If love and truth shed down their genial light.

Oft as I passed their dwellings frail and rude,
   In the chill silence of a wintry night,
Have I entranced in deep attention stood
   And heard, with mingling wonder and delight,

Their hymns of praise, whose music, sweetly wild,
Fell like reproof on Heaven's more favor'd child.

Remnants of mighty tribes and warlike bands,
    I look with sorrow on your swift decay ;
Strangers possess your wide ancestral lands,—
    Like the spring snows your numbers melt away.
Your day of bright historic fame is o'er ;
The regal sceptre ye shall sway no more.

For, as the hemlock sinks in slow decay,
    When the dark forest folds not in its shade,
These forest children droop and pass away,
    Where'er the sturdy Saxon's home is made.
I cast this chaplet on a nation's grave,
And mourn the fate from which we cannot save.

This is the moonless midnight of the year,
    The reign of terror to the struggling poor.
Each freezing gust sounds doleful in their ear,
    As winds that howl across a barren moor
Sound doubly drear, so poverty gives power
To the stern rigors of the wintry hour.

Go to the home of poverty, which Care
    And shivering Want invade, where Joy has fled,
And vanquished Hope surrendered to Despair,—
    Where artless children ask in vain for bread,
Which love and grief are helpless to supply—
Can sadder picture moisten Pity's eye ?

If Heaven has blest, withhold not thou relief;
    They suffer most who most sincerely love ;
Their tender sympathy gives power to grief,
    As trees with branches thickly interwove,
Together bend before the blast, so those
Whom love unites are pierced by common woes.

Beware, lest sordid avarice or pride
    Congeal thy heart against a brother's woes ;
For selfish love can turn compassion's tide
    To ice, and Justice from her throne depose,—
Can steel thy heart with ruthless words to blame,
And bribe thy memory to forget his claim.

Contemn not Poverty, her rugged hand
    Oft nurtures energy to strength sublime ;
And gives to earth those kingly souls, that stand
    The stars that gem the firmament of time ;
The noontide sunshine wilts the fairest flower;
But wintry rigors nerve the frame with power.

Who sway the senates of the world, and mould
    A nation's energy, to wear the form
And impress of their regal thoughts? Who hold
    The helm, and guide the vessel through the storm ?
Who touch the lyre with weird, mysterious art,
And leave their names enshrined in every heart ?

Not hearts besotted with luxurious ease,
    Whose highest boast is vain ancestral pride,

But oftener he whom wealth unheeding sees
　Stemming alone hard fortune's adverse tide,
Battling with frowning fate, till Heaven bestows
　The crown of triumph over vanquished foes.

Then learns the world a lesson, often told,
　That not the pageantry of rank or name,—
The lofty lineage or the hoarded gold,
　Nor boasted legends of ancestral fame,
Can levy homage as their lawful due ;
But mental power to right and goodness true.

Lone child of sorrow, in misfortune's shade,
　Yield not to grief, nor melt thy soul in tears ;
Let not Despair thy strength and peace invade,
　Nor sink desponding in a cloud of fears :
Though gathering darkness hides the sun from sight,
The stars still sparkle on the brow of Night.

Within thy soul remains a sacred place,
　Where Peace and Hope may still serenely dwell ;
And God will give thee all-sufficient grace,
　To rise victorious over earth and hell—
To turn earth's evils into springs of joy,
And all the assailants of thy peace destroy.

No outward fortunes, which the weak control,
　Can the true history of thy life decree ;
The hidden tide, that flows within thy soul,
　Determines all that life will be to thee :

If chained to earth, then earthly ills have power—
If linked to heaven, true peace shall be thy dower.

Problems no finite thought can comprehend,
   With clouds betimes the stars of faith may hide—
O! why does Death strike with his fatal wand
   The cherished idols of our love and pride?
And crush to dust the palaces most grand
   And fair, which Hope had built beautified?
Or why does sin the noblest natures stain,
And spread its shadows o'er the clearest brain?

And why do Passion, Ignorance, and Doubt
   Scatter their hellish seed, in life's spring prime,
And reap rich harvests, o'er which demons shout—
   Harvests of misery, remorse, and crime—
Rank sheaves of ruin, grief, and bootless care,
And bitter, blasted apples of despair?

Why is our bliss so marred with base alloy?
   Why fade the first, the fairest flowers that bloom?
Why are temptations lurking to destroy?
   Why is the world beyond the yawning tomb,
The land of beauty and immortal joy,
   Wrapt in the shadows of mysterious gloom?
In vain I ask. Time shall at length unveil
Those cloud-capt peaks, no mortal foot can scale.

Doubtless the first of Adam's race, who saw
   The wintry rigor of a northern clime,

When Summer's glory, owning Nature's law,
 Vanished, might deem he saw the end of time.
As faded flowers in dust forgotten lay,
And singing birds, in terror, fled away—

When hills and vales wore shrouds of ermine snow,
 And lakes and rivers bound in icy chains,
Well might he weep, with deep despairing woe,
 O'er leafless forests and o'er lifeless plains;
Nor hope, nor dream, that from this frigid tomb,
Unharm'd, the world should rise in vernal bloom.

What rapture thrill'd his wond'ring breast, when Spring
 Waved o'er the desert scene her potent wand!
Again the bowers with dulcet music ring;
 And leaves, and flowers, and streams, at her command,
Their vanish'd beauty to the world restore
Anew, till earth seems fairer than of yore.

And cannot He, who, in the sterile womb
 Of winter, hides the balmy fertile spring,
From life's fierce conflicts, and perplexing gloom—
 From doubt and death, in heaven's bright spring-time,
  bring
The flowers and fruits of shadeless joy and love,
To bloom unfading in the bowers above?

Then trembling pilgrim, needlessly dismayed,
 Let faith in God rebuke thy weak despair;
Though life appears with wintry clouds arrayed,
 Hope on: the spring will dawn serenely fair;

And purer joys shall swell thy grateful breast,
When storms subside and thine is tranquil rest.

Ye youthful hearts, to toil and sorrow born,
  Who scan the future with distrustful eye,
Heed not the brainless sneer, nor envy's scorn—
  Dig deep, where bright and precious diamonds lie :
Live not for earthly crowns of venial praise—
Scale the high mount where golden glories blaze ;
And leave the crowds whom selfish cares immure,
Where darkness lingers and where mists obscure.

If loyal to thy destiny, on earth
  Thou dost thy race with patient courage run,
Unsinning spirits of celestial birth
  Shall hail thee brother, when thy work is done :
Thy darkest hours shall brightest shine above,
Transformed to tokens of thy Father's love.

Philosophy is neither deep nor wise,
  Whose highest truths are present ease or pain :
Are there no chords unseen by her dim eyes,
  Like nerves united to the thoughtful brain,
Which link our spirits to the Father-Soul ?
Has Death no secrets Time can not unroll ?

O Death ! mysterious messenger of Heaven !
  The sternest hearts cannot unmoved behold
The trophies of thy power : to spirits riven
  With sorrow's agony thy heart is cold ;

The cherish'd darling, kindly fate had given,
    To be the light of happiness untold,
From thy fell stroke not Love, nor Hope can save,
Nor tears of anguish that bedew his grave.

The bravest hearts at thy approach must quail,
    If Faith's pure light burn not within the soul ;
Gold, rank, or pleasure, can no more avail,
    Nor earth's philosophy the heart console,—
Nor deepest lore evade the stern decree,
Breath'd to the soul, relentless Power by thee.

'Tis thine to unscale the dimness of the eye,—
    To unseal the deafness of the spirit's ear,—
To break the fetters in which mortals sigh,
    And ope the portals of a deathless sphere,
Where chainless thought shall sweep on tireless wing,
And Love and Joy immortal anthems sing.

Now higher up the sapphire steeps of heaven,
    As days flit past, the sun is seen to shine ;
All hail with joy the cheering token given,
    That Spring will soon, with noiseless fingers, twine
Her wreaths of beauty on the naked hills,
And loose the fetters of imprisoned rills.

Stern, rugged Winter, altho' some were sad,
    Yet many an hour of gladness hast thou seen :
The Earth, in stainless bridal vestments clad,
    Rivals herself in robes of summer green ;

And swampy paths, in summer seldom pass'd,
Are bridged and levell'd by thy drifting blast.

The happy Christmas with its social cheer—
    The nightly converse with the gifted dead—
The merry greetings of the glad New-year—
    The bracing breeze, which health and beauty fed,
When youthful hearts, with buoyant vigor warm,
Beat wild and strong, responsive to the storm :

Like some dark phantom, that unnerves our hearts,
    And flings its shadows o'er the path of life,
Rude Winter comes, untaught in gentle arts,
    And harshest rigor through his reign is rife—
Not with the noiseless, slipper'd foot of Spring,
Not with the tranquil joys the autumns bring :

Yet, when our feet have gained the distant spot,
    Which Fancy painted in the darkest guise,
Our weak forebodings vanish, quite forgot;
    In actual grapple fancied evil flies ;
And fears, which once gave birth to base dismay,
When face to face, like vapors melt away.

How oft the traveller, 'neath his burden bent,
    Journeying o'er ways by him untrod before,
With fainting heart beholds the steep ascent,
    And thinks of hours of climbing toil in store ;
But, when the dreaded height at last is near'd,
    The frowning steep from sight has disappeared ;

Else, finds some winding path, thro' pleasant glades,
Which baseless fancy had with gloom array'd.

All doubt and faithless fear unmans our strength—
 Betrays the trembling spirit to its foes;
But patient toil shall win success at length,
 Whatever obstacles or ills oppose.
Heaven's changeless promise rings forever free,
That as thy days thy strength shall ever be.

My soul, let this thy waning courage stay—
 In hours of gloom and danger, God is near:
He shall the sorrows of thy life allay—
 Safe to the goal, through storm and darkness, steer—
Each frowning barrier from thy way remove,
And lead in hidden paths of truth and love.

THE END.

www.ingramcontent.com/pod-product-compliance
Lightning Source LLC
Chambersburg PA
CBHW030802020726
47499CB00006B/1735